W9-ASE-918

SHOW US WHO YOU ARE

ALSO BY ELLE McNICOLL

A KIND OF SPARK

SHOW US WHO YOU ARE

ELLE McNICOLL

CROWN BOOKS FOR YOUNG READERS
NEW YORK

This is a work of fiction. Names, characters, places, and incidents either are the product of the author's imagination or are used fictitiously. Any resemblance to actual persons, living or dead, events, or locales is entirely coincidental.

 Published in the United States by Crown Books for Young Readers, an imprint of Random House Children's Books, a division of Penguin Random House LLC, New York. Originally published in the United Kingdom and in trade paperback by Knights Of Ltd., London, in 2021.

Crown and the colophon are registered trademarks of Penguin Random House LLC.

Visit us on the Web! rhcbooks.com

Educators and librarians, for a variety of teaching tools, visit us at RHTeachersLibrarians.com

Library of Congress Cataloging-in-Publication Data is available upon request.
ISBN 978-0-593-56299-4 (hardcover) — ISBN 978-0-593-56300-7 (lib. bdg.) —
ISBN 978-0-593-56301-4 (ebook)

The text of this book is set in 12-point Horley Old Style MT Pro.
Interior design by Jen Valero

Printed in the United States of America
1st Printing
First American Edition

To beloved absent friends.

To every helper during the COVID-19 pandemic.
Every small, unspoken sacrifice. Every brave face.
Every quiet breakdown. Thank you for going through
dark times, however that looked.

Nobody is a statistic. To the neurodivergent community.
Thank you for making this a world worth fighting for
just by being you. No test needs to be passed.
No bar met. You are enough.

"Do you know what makes you different, Cora? Could you tell us?"

I don't answer the question immediately. Instead, I look around the room. It's as white, and as clean, as the inside of a bathtub. One large mirror on the wall to my right. Adrien warned me that this place was all smoke and mirrors. Whatever that means.

"Cora?"

I look back in her direction, not making eye contact. Dr. Gold is different. Not like the other scientists that work here. She laughs with her whole body and has a glow about her.

She is smiling at me, awaiting my answer.

They're super smart, but no one can be clever about everything. Adrien told me about them. Prepared me. His dad runs this facility and Adrien has sat right in this chair. In the uncomfortable spot that I'm currently fidgeting in. He's answered the questions.

I can do this too.

Adrien. Adrien is my best friend. And I'm doing all this for him.

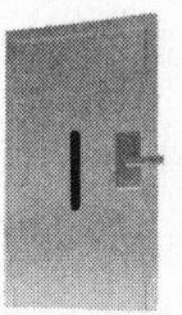

THE DREADED PARTY IN KNIGHTSBRIDGE

A FEW MONTHS EARLIER

"I don't see why I have to come with you both," I say, scowling at my older brother, Gregor, and my dad as they rush me out the front door and into our junky old car.

"It's this little thing called the law, Cora," Dad says as he cheerfully pushes me into the backseat while Gregor frantically checks his reflection in the rearview mirror. "I'm not allowed to leave you alone in the house. Especially after what you did to the toaster."

"The guy from the fire department said that happens all the time. Besides, you're going to let me run around London by myself during the summer," I argue.

The engine starts and we back out onto the road, setting off for the posh part of town. "That's way more dangerous than our house. People drive like maniacs nowadays."

"Don't I know it," Gregor mutters as Dad flies over a

speed bump, causing my brother and me to grab our armrests and hold on for dear life.

The evening lights of London are too bright for me after an absolutely rubbish day at school. I flick the tension out of my fingers and close my eyes. I am in no mood to put on a social mask and try to appear interested in all the boring things the grown-ups are going to say.

Thirteen soon. My, that's a big girl. So *sad about your mother, we heard all about it.*

No, thank you.

Soon enough, Dad and Gregor are bickering about where to park and I realize that we are almost there. Gregor shoves a hastily wrapped present into my hands as we reach the stoop of the enormously tall, but extremely narrow, town house, with a few balloons tied on the doorknob.

"Whose birthday is this?" I hiss as Gregor rings the doorbell.

"Rule Britannia" plays as soon as he does, and Dad has to clap a hand over my mouth to cover my sarcastic groan.

"Save the attitude for later," Gregor hisses back.

"Oh, I will."

"It's the son of my boss. He's your age. Give the present to the maid."

"The *maid*?!"

The black front door is heaved open to reveal . . . a maid. She looks exhausted and thoroughly unamused. Music and conversation and crowds of people can be seen and heard just behind her. Dad hastily drops his hand from my face as I thrust the present toward her. She accepts it with a sigh and turns to add it to a gigantic pyramid of fancily wrapped gifts.

We follow her in, and she takes our coats. Dad and Gregor are both wearing suits that make them look like very nervous penguins.

"Gregory!"

My brother rushes off to answer to someone who has gotten his name wrong, leaving Dad and me standing in the hallway. Dad runs his hands along his lapels anxiously while I stare around at the incredibly posh house.

I'm scared to touch anything; it's like a museum.

"Who are you, then?"

I glance up at a tall, willowy woman with long icy-blond hair as she descends the stairs gracefully. She's holding her hand out toward me with a wide smile.

It's moments like these when I have no idea what they want me to do. Does she want me to hold her hand or shake it?

I gingerly put out my hand and her bracelets jangle as she grasps it. Squeezes it.

"Are you a friend of Adrien's?" she asks excitedly.

"No. I'm Cora Byers. My brother works for Mr. Hawkins."

"And Mr. Hawkins has been incredibly rude and stolen

your brother away from you and your father when you don't know a soul," she says, smiling brightly at Dad.

She's still gripping my hand. "Yes," I answer bluntly.

She laughs.

"You come with me, my love," she says, leading me through the swarm of people, who pay us no attention. Hollow laughter rings out around me as the lady leads me to the back of the house. "There aren't a lot of kiddies here for you to talk to, I'm afraid."

"Oh." I don't tell her that I actually don't mind being by myself.

"Please get Mr. Byers a drink," she tells the maid as we pass her.

"Can't, I'm driving," Dad calls before disappearing into the crowd behind us.

We reach what must be the back door and she finally releases my hand.

"See if you can find the birthday boy," she says, handing me a large, shining golden key that was hanging on the wall. I stare down at it in confusion, and then back up at her, but she's gone. Leaving me with the mysterious item.

The back door is already open, so I'm not certain what the key is for until I step outside.

Down the stone steps, I can see it. A huge, hidden garden, behind tall iron gates, with trees peeking over the top. I move slowly toward it, desperate for the solitude and quiet. I can't stand the crowded bodies, the noise and all the sensory pressure.

A garden seems so luxurious. I wish we had one.

The key opens the black gate swiftly and I'm inside, sheltered by the trees.

A biology teacher at school said something about trees and oxygen; I can't fully remember the lesson. But I do feel like they give me breath sometimes.

I'm just starting to feel relaxed when I get a tingle. I'm being followed.

Constantly having trouble in the school hallways has given me a sixth sense. I know when I'm being watched or talked about. I can feel the unwanted attention on the back of my neck.

I keep walking, gripping the key and pressing it against my stomach. Maybe it's because I had a nasty day at school, but I'm quickly becoming angry.

I'm tired of being treated like a spectacle.

As I hear a faint crunch behind me, I spin around. I slam my arm against the blur of a shape and push.

It falls to the ground, taking me down too, the key forgotten on the grass by the path.

"Hey!"

My forearm is pressed against the collarbone of a boy. My age, or a little older. He splutters for a moment and then laughs loudly.

"Why are you creeping up on me?" I snap.

"Why are you so strong?" he retorts, laughing between words.

"Are you spying on me?"

"Oh, yes," he snorts as I release him. He sits up, still laughing. "You walked all the way from the gate to the middle of the path. Exciting stuff."

"Who are you?"

"You're the one in my garden. You should tell me who you are."

I take a good look at him. Tall but not gangly, and definitely my age. Dark curls and a nose that's a little too big for his face. His eyes are completely lit up with laughter and it's very alarming. All the boys at school have started getting really mean eyes. His are nothing like theirs.

I glare at him. "You're Adrien Hawkins."

He points his finger right in front of my face. "You got it."

I shove his finger away. "Fine. Happy birthday. Your present's back in the house."

"You got me a present?"

"Sure."

"That's nice for a complete stranger."

He doesn't talk like other kids our age. Or any grown-ups I know, in fact. None of my rehearsed and prepared conversations match what he's saying so I just pick up the key and walk away, toward what appears to be tennis courts at the other end of the secret garden.

"Do you go to school?" he asks, falling in step beside me.

"Of course I go to school," I mutter.

"I don't."

"That makes sense," I reply, looking him up and down.

"Why?"

"I dunno." I blow my bangs out of my eyes. "You're not . . . broken down."

He chuckles. "Yeah. Mum pulled me out before that could happen. I learn better at home."

Maybe that's why his behavior is so different.

"Do you have a name?"

"Yes," I say coolly.

"Can you tell me?"

"Why aren't you at your own party?"

"It's not really my party," he says flatly. "It's my dad's party. For all his fancy friends and people from work."

"Your dad's my brother's boss."

"Your brother works at Pomegranate?"

Pomegranate Institute is Magnus Hawkins's company. I'm still not entirely sure what they do there. Gregor sometimes starts talking about it, but Dad always changes the subject.

"Yes," I tell him, happier to talk about Gregor than about myself.

"My dad must think he's useful if he's invited you all here."

Another strange comment. I ignore it.

"It's fine if you don't want to tell me your name."

"Good."

"I'll just guess."

I close my eyes. Is he going to go through every girl's name he can think of?

"Angela." He is.

"Bryony?"

Alphabetically.

"It's Cora." I sigh.

"C for Cora." He grins. "Cool. I like that."

I keep waiting for a horrid remark to follow. That's what the kids at school would do. Sweetness followed by an even bigger sting. But he doesn't.

Mum once said, when she was alive, that boys were mean to girls because they liked them. I thought that was the most revolting thing I had ever heard, and I know it's not true of the boys at school.

Adrien suddenly turns his head and whistles, loudly and shrilly. I flinch away from him, the sound too loud for my senses.

Something comes bounding toward us. "Cerby, this is Cora. Cora, this is my dog."

A large dog with tufty ears looks up at me, tail wagging furiously.

"Boy, she had me pinned to the ground and where were you?" Adrien asks jokingly, ruffling the dog's neck fur. "Huh? Where were you?"

I fight a smile and lose. The dog is cute, and they make a nice pair.

"I want to see this present Cora's brought all the way here for me, boy," Adrien says teasingly. He sets off toward the house, Cerby following him diligently.

I scowl. He's calling my bluff and I don't like it.

I follow the two of them out of the garden and up the stone steps to the back door of the house. Everyone seems to have moved into the drawing room. The birthday present pile remains untouched by the stairs.

Adrien moves toward it and then glances over at me. "So. Which one is from you?"

I grimace, trying to remember. Then I spot the one that hasn't been professionally gift-wrapped. "That one." He carefully whips it out and the pyramid stays intact.

I'm almost impressed.

"It's signed from you and Gregor," he states, smiling as he reads the tag. "So what is it?"

He stares at me straight-on, lips twitching. I glower.

I'm not losing this annoying game.

"It's"—I try to think of which boring yet useful thing my big brother would have bought and wrapped up—"it's an alarm clock."

"An alarm clock?" He slowly pulls the ribbon from the

box, never looking away from me and never losing his determined little smile. "Really?"

I smile back haughtily. "Really."

Adrien unwraps the package, gaze still locked onto me. I suddenly feel like snorting.

He's making me laugh.

We both look down, surprised to see him unwrapping a model plane in a box. One that has to be built from scratch. I look up at him, expecting him to gloat at the fact that he won our odd little back-and-forth.

But he looks suddenly less playful.

"Sorry," I say jokingly. "Not an alarm clock."

"No, this is better," he says quietly. "I love planes."

I look down at Cerby, who's sniffing the other presents. "Well . . . that's good."

"I want to be a pilot someday," he tells me, smiling widely.

"Wow." I want to be a reporter, but I don't say so out loud.

He puts the box gently on top of the pile and beams at me.

"Thanks, Cora. I *love* my present."

I snort, knowing he knows I had no part in the present. But I want to pretend I did, so I smile graciously. "You're welcome, Adrien."

"You found him!"

We both turn to see the glamorous woman from earlier.

She comes over, a glass of champagne in one of her slender hands.

"Come here!"

Adrien pretends to try to escape her, but she catches him and plants a huge wet kiss on his temple. She leaves a massive dark red lipstick stain on his skin and he laughs. "Happy birthday, darling." She keeps one arm wrapped around him, turning to smile warmly at me.

"Cora! Did you like the garden?"

"Yeah," I say, a little shyly. "Yeah, it was nice."

"And have you two made friends, then?" she asks brightly, looking back at Adrien.

I expect him to be embarrassed and to pull away from her, but he beams broadly at me. "Yep."

I'm too surprised to argue.

"Good!" his mum cries delightedly. Her happiness is too obvious to mistake or misread. "Adrien gets quite lonesome during the summers, Cora. You must come over whenever you want."

I think of my own usually long and lonely summers and feel a strange twinge.

"I'll think about it, Mrs. Hawkins."

And the weird thing is that I just might.

2 THE POMEGRANATE INSTITUTE

It's Saturday, the day after the party. I'm sitting at our breakfast table and Gregor has made me a plate of buttery toast and two large fried eggs. Dad is staring out the window, as he does now that Mum isn't here to tell him off for putting too much salt on his eggs. Gregor is reading the newspaper.

"What does Pomegranate do?"

I ask Gregor the question. Dad glances at me nervously.

"It's not easy to explain," Gregor says carefully, laying his newspaper down with an air of great importance. "They use artificial intelligence to provide a service."

"Like robots?"

"No, not robots. More like holograms."

"Gregor." Dad's voice is a warning.

"What are they holograms of?" I ask Gregor, ignoring Dad.

"Well, they're of people," Gregor says. "Of real people."

I frown in confusion. "I don't understand."

"When it's fully up and running"—Gregor scoots his chair a little closer to me and gives me his full attention—"it will be open to the paying public. They can pay money to spend time with the holograms."

"But why would they do that?"

"Well, because some of them will be doubles of famous people. They can pay money and have a long conversation with their favorite actor or musician. Like they're really meeting the person."

"But how will that be like meeting the real thing?"

"Well, that's where the Golden Department comes in. They take great pains to make sure every Gram—hologram, that is—will be as humanlike and true to life as possible. They'll study the subject they're re-creating and won't activate the Gram until it's identical. It's people's brains and souls uploaded onto a computer and then projected!"

Gregor is so proud to work for Pomegranate. I can tell he's thrilled that I'm finally asking questions. I look at Dad, who is glaring into his mug of coffee.

"It sounds interesting," I say.

"Well, that's just part of it. The real work of it will be—"

"Enough!" Dad snaps, getting to his feet and clearing his place at the table. "You've told her about that place, let's talk about something else."

"What's the real work?" I demand. I hate when they keep things from me. Gregor is so much older than me, he's twenty-six and I'm just twelve, so they've always outnumbered me with their infuriating grown-upness.

"Well, we interview real people and study them so that we can make a Gram of them and then they can live forever. Virtually. Like virtual immortality. Then their loved ones can visit them after they've died."

I stare at Gregor. Processing what it is he's just said. "So . . ." I feel all the things I want to say jumbled up inside me. "So, if Mum had been interviewed and studied by this place, they could have made a copy of her to live forever?"

Dad makes a sound I can't name and storms out of the room, but Gregor smiles a watery smile. "Exactly, Cora."

The idea is so strange, it frightens me a little.

"Speaking of Pomegranate, there's something I actually wanted to talk to you about," Gregor says, glancing at the door to the hall as if he expects Dad to come charging back in.

"What?"

"You see, Magnus . . . you know, the guy whose house we were at last night."

Adrien's dad. "Yes?"

"He's really interested in interviewing you for the Golden Department."

I flinch. "What? Why?"

"Right now, his team is really good at re-creating neurotypical people, but he'd love to get a realistically autistic Gram."

I freeze. We never talk about me being autistic. I don't know why, I don't see anything wrong with it. I was sent to a psychiatrist before Mum died and he ended up diagnosing me. That was a while ago now, and Dad and Gregor haven't brought it up since. I sometimes wonder if they've forgotten. "I don't get it."

"Well, they want the holograms to be as accurate and lifelike as possible," Gregor explains. "And, because autistic people are much rarer than neurotypical people, they haven't mastered how to replicate that kind of brain yet."

"I . . ." I feel very exposed talking about this. "I would just need to be interviewed a bunch of times?"

"It doesn't matter." Dad suddenly enters the room, his coat on and his eyes furious. "Because you're not doing it. You hear me, Gregor? She's not doing that."

"Dad." Gregor's voice is steely as they have a secret conversation with their eyes. I glance down at the linoleum, uncomfortable.

"Dad, Magnus would pay a lot of money for her input."

"I don't care. It's not happening. Tell your boss, who can't even get your name right, that your little sister won't be one of his guinea pigs."

"Dad, this thing is so huge! So much more important than you can understand right now. People will be able to grieve properly. Heck, they won't have to grieve at all! They won't ever have to say goodbye, unless they want to. It's remarkable stuff."

"You can say that until the cows come home, son, but she's having nothing to do with it. Not for all the gold in Egypt. No. She's not an experiment."

I watch Dad leave the house while Gregor storms upstairs to his room. As two doors slam, I slowly clear my plate. I stare at the white china as it gets steadily cleaner and I wonder what it must be like. To see someone come back to life in the form of a hologram.

I can't understand Dad's reaction. Surely it must be the most wonderful idea in the world.

Never having to say goodbye to somebody.

NOT A GOOD FIT

I'm usually very distracted at school. I don't find it an easy environment at all. Especially since my best friend, Zoe, moved to Australia. We try to video call when we can, but the time difference is massive and Zoe was never good with schedules.

I'm alert today, though. As we only have a few weeks left before the summer holidays, Mr. Ramsey is announcing the editorial team for the newspaper next term. I've wanted to be an investigative journalist since the day I found out that it was a real job. It's all I've been focused on these last few weeks. I've written sample stories, researched projects, proofread practice papers, and put together a front-page layout to show off my plans and ideas.

Dad said that to get the job you want, you have to go the extra mile.

So I went an extra marathon.

"All right, one final thing before you make a break for

it." Mr. Ramsey hops up onto his desk, puts his glasses on and picks up a piece of paper. I lean forward, knowing the moment has finally arrived. "Next year's newspaper. Thank you for your entries and for your interviews, those of you who applied. Ms. Mabuse and I were thoroughly impressed by the high standard."

I glance over at our teaching assistant, Ms. Mabuse, who smiles kindly at me.

"However, not everyone can make the cut. I've got our two editors and our three writers, and they are as follows . . ."

I hold my breath. I tell myself, silently, that I'll be happy just to make the team. I don't have to be an editor, I'll just be happy to make the team.

"Editors, Jack and Michael. Reporters . . . Gemma, Kate and Paul."

Most of the class leap to their feet to escape the room as soon as his announcement is over, but I am stuck, stunned, in my seat.

I stagger to my feet and sweep all my things into my backpack. I feel a touch on my elbow and jerk in surprise.

It's Ms. Mabuse.

"Cora, I want you to know that I read your entire submission folder and your work is exemplary."

She smiles at me, sadly.

I puff out a breath. "Thank you, Ms. Mabuse."

"I recommended that you be chosen." She says it so softly. As if it's a secret.

I make my way to Mr. Ramsey's desk, feeling like I'm coming out of a dream.

"Mr. Ramsey?"

"Yes, Cora?"

"Um . . ." I wait until the final members of the class have filed out of the room. "Can I ask something?"

"You can and you may."

"Why didn't I make the newspaper team?"

He sighs and looks up at me. His expression is a grimace, an awful mask of pity. "Cora . . . I really appreciated the effort that you made in your application, but I had to go for the most qualified team."

"I know that." I can feel my own mask starting to slip. "That's what you said when you told us to apply. You said it was going to be really hard work and not to waste your time if we weren't serious about it."

"I can tell you were serious about it, don't worry, Cora." Mr. Ramsey chuckles.

"But I did extra work," I maintain, feeling both embarrassed and indignant. "And I'm sorry, but Michael and Paul both got their articles from the internet. From another writer, I saw them do it during Computer Studies."

I never tattle on people, but I'm boiling in exasperation.

"Cora, look. You have enough to deal with at the moment, I don't think putting you on the paper would be good for you."

"Mr. Ramsey"—my voice trembles a little—"if I

thought this was going to be too much for me, I wouldn't have applied. Also"—I don't know what has possessed me, but I go on—"almost all the interviewees were girls, but you've let in every boy who applied. How does a paper end up with a sixty-percent-male staff, when eighty percent of the applicants were female?"

I can see him trying to do the sum in his head. He gives up and rubs the back of his neck. "The boys who applied aren't that serious about their work at present. This opportunity would be really good for them. Something for them to commit to. I was thrilled they even applied!"

"So then just say that, Mr. Ramsey," I say hoarsely, hating myself for getting so worked up. "Say that they need it more. Or that you like them more. Don't say that they earned it more, especially if you can't prove it."

"Cora." His tone is steely, and I can't really blame him. I don't usually talk back to teachers. "Stop it. Being on the paper is about more than just hard work, you know that. It's also about teamwork. That's true for the real world as well. People usually want to hire folks that they can get along with and have a nice time with, okay? It's about personality as much as talent."

I look down to see my hand clenching the desk, knuckles flushed. "So it doesn't matter how good you are. It's not about skill."

"Hey now." He smiles gently at me, and I know he probably believes he's being really understanding right now. "No point in getting upset. These things happen. There will be other opportunities."

"I worked so hard, Mr. Ramsey. I'm not saying I'm entitled to anything, I just know this isn't fair."

I feel so stupid. I can't base facts on feelings, I know, but I can just feel that this isn't right. I didn't feel entitled to win at Sports Day. I know how rubbish I am at throwing and catching. I didn't feel I deserved a medal just for showing up and trying. They tried to give me one once, for coming in last in the two-hundred-meter sprint, and I refused to take it. I didn't demand to know why I wasn't let into the school choir. I know my singing voice is horrendous.

I accepted all those because I knew I wasn't good enough. But I know I'm good enough for this. I *know* I am. "Why would you think I couldn't work well in a team, Mr. Ramsey?"

"Oh, Cora." He gives me the same infuriatingly pitying smile. "You know why. Your condition . . . well . . . I wouldn't want you to be overwhelmed. I just don't think you're a good fit for it."

I feel a cold sweat between my shoulder blades. Righteous anger that makes it impossible for me to speak. Making eye contact is completely unthinkable.

He picks up his coffee cup and squeezes my shoulder briefly before leaving the classroom. I flinch at the contact, not in the space or mood to tolerate it.

The faraway, bustling sounds of the school carrying on

without me echo in the hallway. I stare at my fingers, still gripping the desk for dear life.

"Are you all right?"

My head shoots up. Ms. Mabuse is standing in the doorway, holding a sandwich and a bottle of water.

"I'm fine," I lie.

I just want to be heard. I just want a way to be understood. I feel like people read me all wrong, and if I had a way to put the thoughts down and send them out into the world, then they wouldn't. Then they would understand.

"Oh, come on." Ms. Mabuse kicks the door shut with her foot and pulls up a chair to sit in. "I'd be furious if I were you."

I smile quickly and haul my backpack over my shoulder. "It's nothing."

"Cora, if you ever want to talk about anything, I'm right here."

"Thanks." I move to the door, letting my long hair fall across my face to hide my expression. "I'm fine, though."

I never know how to explain. The feeling can flow through a pen, but never through my voice.

*

I'm still processing and mulling over the whole thing as I walk home. The June sunshine feels oppressive.

That's what Mum used to call it. She couldn't stand the warmth.

"CORA!"

I glance up. Across the road, it's him. Adrien. The boy from the party.

He waves enthusiastically, a grin spread wide across his face. He starts heading toward me, narrowly avoiding a car in the process. The driver rolls down his window to yell something, but Adrien is completely oblivious. He jogs over to me while all I can do is stare.

I don't like changes to my routine. Today has been disruptive enough. I wonder if I can run away.

"Don't run away." This surprises me. People usually aren't able to read my thoughts.

"Hey." I fix him with what I hope is my scariest expression. "Don't tell me what to do, I've had an awful day."

"All school days are awful. You should come and be taught at my house instead."

"No thanks." I start off again, walking toward my street.

"Do you always walk home alone?"

"Yes, I prefer it that way."

"You prefer being alone."

I stop and deliberately look him up and down. "Absolutely."

He laughs.

"So, what are you doing down here anyway?" I ask, comforted by the knowledge that I'm not far from home. "This is a long way from Snob Hill."

I expect him to be offended but he laughs again.

Irritatingly.

"Snob Hill? You don't like Knightsbridge?"

"Do you?"

He seriously considers the question. "I like it enough."

"Really? Where people lock up their gardens and ignore their maids?"

"Her name's Bella and I don't ignore her."

I reach my street and quicken my pace. "Well, good for you."

"Hey, I came to ask you something."

I was so close to safety. I roll my eyes and fumble in my bookbag for my key. "What?"

"My mum's garden party is this weekend and she said I could invite a friend."

I stare at him, waiting for the question. "And?"

"And I'm inviting you."

"Right." I jam my key in the lock and turn to give him my full attention. "Is this meant to be a joke?"

"No."

"We don't know each other."

"Cora, that's very hurtful. You got me that beautiful model airplane."

I scowl. "We aren't friends. What's wrong with you?"

Something flashes across his face, something sad, but it disappears just as quickly. "I'd *like* to be friends."

"You can't just follow someone around and make them be your friend."

"Why not?"

"Because"—I fight every little voice in my head whispering that he's right—"it's not normal."

"And you care about normal?"

No.

"Yes," I snap. Mr. Ramsey's earlier treatment of me is still smarting, still hurting. "I do. I've decided that I really care about normal."

"You shouldn't," he says, grinning. "I've tried all that, it's why I'm homeschooled now."

"You didn't really come all the way down here to see me, did you?"

"Well, no, not exactly," he replies, turning to point to the corner of the road. "That shop is called Flight. They sell all kinds of stuff to do with airplanes. I'm pretty sure it's where your brother got my birthday gift from. I come here quite a bit, actually."

"Ah, that's a little less creepy. Thanks."

I suddenly notice a black car pulling up and parking on the end of our cul-de-sac. I squint to see if I recognize the driver. Adrien sees me looking and glances back.

"That's our chauffeur," he tells me. "He follows me while I follow people."

"Yeah, I'm not sure I want any new friends right now. Especially not spoiled rich ones."

He looks at me for a moment and then looks up at my house. I bristle. It's small and modest and I'm ready to defend it ferociously.

"I like your house."

I release all my puffed-up air when I hear how genuine he sounds.

"Can I come in?"

I look back at his driver. "Jeeves won't mind?"

"Nope. And his name's Lloyd. As long as I'm home before Dad, it'll be fine. And Dad is never home before nine on a weekday."

I weigh it all up in my head and then exhale. "Fine. Come in."

He happily falls into step with me and we go into my house. He makes no effort to hide his nosiness. He stares at all our photographs on the wall. Peers into the living room. Then follows me down the hallway into the kitchen. I dump my backpack on the counter and open the fridge. I drink some orange juice from the carton and then grab a bottle of water.

"I really like your house."

"Thanks."

"It's really lived-in."

I remember thinking that his house looked like a museum. Or a show home.

"Where is everyone?" he asks after a pause.

"My brother stays late at Pomegranate too," I tell him. "And Dad drops by the pub down the road around this time. I'm home earlier than normal."

Dad has finally got over the toaster incident, so I'm allowed to be home by myself now.

"And your mum?"

My hand slips as I try to open my bottle of water. "She's dead."

There is usually a sticky silence when I tell people this. It's awkward and embarrassing, like I've trapped them somehow by making them uncomfortable over someone in my family dying.

"That's horrible."

I look up at him. He actually looks sorry, not uncomfortable or anxious.

"Thanks. It was over a year ago now."

"Still horrible."

Now I'm the one who feels a bit awkward. I don't like social situations, I'm not naturally great at them. It often feels like everyone else has been running lines for weeks before I arrived and we're about to be pushed out onstage. I stumble and try my best, while everyone else stares at me like I'm letting them all down.

I've tried for years to perfect my social interactions and predict how people will respond and behave. I've gotten better at it, I don't go wrong that often anymore.

People, normal people, are all quite conventional and unsurprising.

Adrien never responds like other people. He's unpredictable.

I have a stray thought, but I push it away. It's far too unlikely.

"Why was today such a bad day?"

I wonder if I should actually tell him. It will probably sound so silly to him. Other kids never seem to be quite so intense, or so serious. They rarely understand why I care about certain things so much, or why I have a hard time letting some things go. Even Zoe sometimes sighs and asks me why I fixate on things the way I do.

"I worked really hard to get a position on next year's school newspaper team," I hear myself saying, bluntly. "And my teacher said I wouldn't be a good fit."

I regret saying it. Now he's going to ask how I know that I worked harder than the others, how I know I would have been a good fit. He's going to wonder why I would even want extra work at school in the first place.

"That's partly why Mum let me learn at home. They make everything so much harder if you're different."

I stare at him. It's not what I'm used to hearing. I feel caught off guard by it, actually.

"Why would you think I'm different?" I ask, a little defensive but also nervous.

"Different" can seem like a fun personality trait to some people.

But for me, it feels like being caught.

We stare at each other for a moment and I don't know what to say.

"Hello?"

We both turn to see Dad arriving home. He is clearly stunned to see Adrien here. Adrien smiles cheerfully and waves. "Hi, Mr. Byers."

"Dad, this is Adrien Hawkins. Remember? From the party?"

"Is that your black Lexus out there, son?"

"Yeah." Adrien nods and holds out his hand. Dad shakes it steadily, glancing at me.

"Is he starting to look antsy out there, Mr. Byers?"

"Well . . . I don't—"

"I'll get going, then. I was just letting Cora know she's invited to our family gathering on Saturday. It's in our garden. Seven o'clock. She has a key."

I'm about to deny it but he's already gone. Walking swiftly but calmly down the hall and out of the front door.

"Strange lad," Dad murmurs as we watch the front door close.

I silently agree, grabbing my backpack to head upstairs.

As I slip it from the counter, a large gold key falls from the front pocket and lands on the linoleum floor.

I pick it up, gingerly. And then slip it into my pocket.

LIKE ME

I can hear the hum of loud and joyous voices as I approach the iron gate leading into the large garden. I feel the same anxious knot in my stomach that I always feel before a social situation. I faintly hear Gregor calling, from the car, that he'll be back at nine for me. I wave him off.

I use the key and enter the garden.

I follow the breeze of conversation to the gathering. I don't see any other children. It doesn't bother me so much; I find both grown-ups and people my age baffling.

And they find me even stranger, usually.

"Cora?"

I jump at the sound of my name and look up at a man. He's so tall that he is blocking my eyes from the sun shining through the trees. His suit is fitted well, it's not like Dad's. He's dressed like a movie star. He has dark circles under his eyes, but laughter lines as well, and dark curly hair with streaks of silver. He watches me expectantly.

"Mr. Hawkins?"

I've never met him, but I recognize him from Gregor's stories. I just know it's him.

"Did Adrien invite you?"

I'm trying so hard not to stare at the grass. I'm trying to meet his gaze, but it feels physically uncomfortable. I wasn't prepared for this introduction and he's very intimidating.

"Yes. Yes, he did."

He nods, smiling. "Good. He needs some chums his own age. You must be Gregory's little sister."

"Gregor . . . yes." I don't hesitate to correct him.

"Has he brought you down to visit the facility yet?"

"No, he hasn't."

"Well, he should. We want it to be more inclusive for young people, marketing would love to hear your opinions."

I'm not sure I fully understand what he's just said but I nod.

"How about tomorrow? Sundays are usually pretty relaxed. Maybe Greg can bring you by?"

It feels more like an order than a question, but I *am* curious about Pomegranate, especially since Gregor told me what they're trying to do.

"I'd like that. I'll ask him."

Magnus Hawkins smiles broadly and for a split second looks a lot like Adrien.

"Have fun at the party, Cora."

He disappears into the crowd of grown-ups and I'm left standing alone. I'm relieved that he didn't make me come and join in. I stand by myself and try to relax a little.

And almost fall to the ground as a panting, excitable dog crashes into my legs.

"Cerby!"

Mrs. Hawkins and Adrien appear at the edge of the garden, Adrien calling after his bounding dog and Mrs. Hawkins laughing. I reach down to scratch Cerby's ears and his wet nose butts against my cheek.

"Was Dad bothering you about Pomegranate?" Adrien demands cheerfully as he and his glamorous mum reach my side.

"He said I could have a look around tomorrow."

"Goodness." Mrs. Hawkins looks over at the crowd, which swallowed up Adrien's dad. "He's usually very selective about who he invites to the facility. He must like you, Cora."

I feel a warmness when she says that. It soothes the pain from Mr. Ramsey's rejection. I've somehow impressed someone. I feel like I've passed a test.

Someone is calling Mrs. Hawkins, so she squeezes my elbow once, quickly, and smiles a beatific smile before scampering away. Her long, swishy white trousers brush against the perfectly mowed grass and her blond hair stays perfectly in place despite the breeze.

"You decided to drop by, then?"

I briefly meet Adrien's gaze before returning my attention to Cerby. I love dogs. They don't like long sustained eye contact either.

"Did my dad say anything else to you?" He sounds . . . nervous.

"No. Just that he'd like my opinion on the Institute. I'm going to go in tomorrow. Apparently it's quieter on Sundays."

"Yes, it is."

He doesn't seem pleased, but I don't know the right question to ask in order to get him to talk about it.

"Want some advice?"

I glance up. "Advice?"

"About Pomegranate."

I reach down and pluck one perfect blade of grass from the ground and squeeze it in my palm. "I'm sure I'll manage."

"Nah, listen." He hunkers down next to me, and Cerby turns his attention to his boy. "It's a weird place. The people, the building . . . it's just weird."

"It's your dad's business," I remind him.

"Yeah, I know."

"So? Don't you want to support him?"

He shifts on the grass, getting comfortable. "He's not the easiest person to support."

I scoff. Magnus Hawkins seems completely easy. He keeps conversations brief and to the point.

Adrien's eyes lock onto mine. "You don't know him like I do."

"Of course I don't," I agree, rolling my eyes. "But one parent always has to be difficult, and the other has to be nice. My dad is one of my best friends. But my mum was always so tough."

He looks surprised and I know why. We're never supposed to say anything even a little bit mean about the dead, we're supposed to remember them as perfect—but no one is perfect.

"I still wish I'd spent more time with her. Now that she's gone. No matter how tough she was."

I don't exactly know why I'm telling him this.

He watches me closely. "You know what it is that they do at Pomegranate?"

I force myself to look at him. Straight-on. "Yes. Gregor told me. I know exactly what they do."

Adrien nods slowly. "Well, all right then. I hope you like it there."

"You've been?"

"Oh, yeah."

"So what was so awful about it?"

"It's not awful," he admits, rubbing Cerby's exposed tummy. "It's full of clever people and they serve good food."

I laugh. I can't help it. He's unexpected and I'm surprised by how much I'm starting to enjoy that.

"I have an idea," he suddenly announces, hopping up to his feet.

"Uh-huh?"

"It's the summer holidays soon."

"In a few weeks."

"Yeah, that's what I said. Soon."

It doesn't feel soon to me. Four weeks in my school seems like an eternity.

"Over summer, we should make our own newspaper."

I blink up at him. His sudden switch in topic feels like Dad's driving. A sudden jerk to the left, unexpectedly. I shake my head and say, "What?"

"We should make our own paper. We'll write the articles, print copies and distribute them around town." Cerby pants loudly, glancing between us as if he can pick up on Adrien's excited energy and my complete bemusement.

"Adrien," I laugh out his name in a burst. "Thanks, but you don't need to make me feel better about the school paper."

He cocks his head slightly and frowns. "That's not what I'm trying to do. I get so bored during the summer. It would be fun. Besides, people aren't used to people like us having the front page."

"People like us? You mean children?"

He smiles, quickly. Then glances back over at the herd of grown-ups. "Yeah. Sure."

"What do you mean 'like us'?"

He turns back to regard me. Smiling. "Well, you *are.*"

"Am what?"

"Like me."

I let out a nervous laugh. "Adrien, I'm not sure anyone is like you."

I'm still not even sure if that is a compliment. He's so unpredictable and frantic. And yet the moments when he is so still are the strangest.

"I'll think about it," I tell him.

"Well." He shrugs happily, grinning. "I'll start thinking of big exposés for us to uncover."

I chuckle and get to my feet. "Hey, maybe I'll find something at Pomegranate tomorrow. We can open with that."

Something flickers for a moment in his face and then disappears. "Yeah. Maybe you will."

HER

The building is at least six stories tall and has been designed to look like an Edwardian town house. It looks tiny and out of place among the cold, crisp skyscrapers of Canary Wharf.

Gregor and I both agreed it was better that Dad didn't know I was going to the Pomegranate Institute today. Dad left for West Brompton Cemetery and Gregor took me to work with him. Now, as I stand on the sidewalk and stare up at the place, I wish Dad were with me.

Usually Canary Wharf is full of people in suits. Black suits, gray suits, navy suits. They bustle around you on the wide sidewalk, all talking to each other or to people on the other ends of their phones. They move at a quick, calculated speed that would knock out anything that crossed their path.

But none of them are here this Sunday. It's a ghost town.

The glass double doors of Pomegranate are opened for

us by a doorman, who nods at my brother with familiarity. The lobby is simple. A reception desk with an elevator to the left and stairs to the right. The receptionist smiles professionally at us, but there's a little curiosity in her eyes as she examines me.

"May I sign my little sister in, Noma? She's visiting today."

Noma gestures toward a light white tablet and an electronic stylus. I'm careful as I sign my name and slide it back. She turns to a little machine and murmurs a command, causing it to zip out a laminated card. Gregor attaches it to a lanyard and hands it to me.

"That's your access key for the day," Noma says slowly. "So don't lose it. 'Kay?"

"Um . . ." I fix it around my neck and nod. "Okay."

"Notice anything about Noma?" Gregor asks me delicately.

I glance back at the receptionist, who is now speaking to somebody on the phone. But she's not holding a receiver or wearing a headset. She stares straight ahead, hands clasped in front of her, and speaks as if the person on the other end is in her head.

"Um." I watch her and then turn to my brother. "She's very intense. And young."

He smiles softly and nods. We set off.

"Want to see my boring office?" Gregor asks me.

"I want to see everything," I say.

Everything is so . . . white. The walls, the carpet, the minimal amounts of furniture. Even the little crystals in the dainty chandelier above me in reception. While outside is silver and gray and chrome, inside it is as clean as snow.

"We'll start on the ground floor, then," Gregor tells me, leading me into the room to the east. "Boring stuff here, I'm afraid. This is the restaurant."

It's posh. Posher than anywhere I've ever eaten. When Gregor described it in the car, I thought it would be like a canteen. But there are linen tablecloths. Soft piano music is playing and the smell in the air is incredible.

"Obviously this will be busy and thriving when we open to the public," Gregor whispers to me.

There are only two people currently eating in the restaurant. I recognize one as Magnus and the other is a woman I've never seen before, not even in Gregor's immersive stories. Magnus looks up from what seems to be a delicious lobster roll to see the two of us. His face morphs into a smile and he stands, beckoning us over.

I dash over to them, dodging the empty tables with their perfectly set silverware.

"Told you Sundays were quiet," Magnus says to me with a wink. "Cora, this is Dr. Gold. She's the resident genius here at Pomegranate."

Dr. Gold. Gregor *has,* as it happens, mentioned her several times.

The Golden Department was named after Dr. Gold. I'm angry at myself for assuming that she was a man.

She's stunning. I don't think much about beauty; I was never fond of Mum's makeup or perfume. I found it all too overpowering in its smell and texture. But I can recognize how truly beautiful Dr. Gold is. Bright eyes, dark lashes, high cheekbones and shiny blond hair. So blond, it's almost white.

"Hello."

I gaze down at her, amazed that the scientist Gregor raved about so much is so far from what I expected.

"Cora is Gregor's sister and a friend of my son's," Magnus tells Dr. Gold. "Against her better judgment, I fear."

Dr. Gold laughs and I feel instantly at ease. It's such an unusual feeling for me. I realize that I'm openly staring at her, so I look at Gregor instead. He beams down at me.

"I invited her for a tour of Pomegranate but I'm a terrible host, I must apologize to you, Cora," Magnus goes on. "I have a video call with my investors, and sadly Americans tend to take up the whole day."

"Poor Americans," chuckles Dr. Gold. "I can give you the tour, my love," she adds, smiling brightly, showing off two rows of perfectly white, straight teeth.

"Okay," I agree eagerly. We smile at each other.

"Ciao for now, then," Magnus says, sitting back down in his chair and withdrawing a paper-thin tablet from his pocket. "Say goodbye before you leave today, Cora." I nod, feeling somewhat important. I follow Dr. Gold back out into reception, making an effort to walk quickly but not so quickly that I step on her heels. Her shoes click and clack against the marble floor and when we reach Noma's desk, she turns and beams at me.

"Not going to find a more interesting room than the restaurant, I'm afraid," she says, talking to me rather than Gregor. "The food is absolutely gorgeous. It's my favorite part of Pomegranate. You must have lunch before you leave. I'd eat their pasta every hour if I had the time."

I giggle. Mum always made comments about my love of food so Dr. Gold's obvious enjoyment of it makes me tingle with joy.

"If we go through here . . ." She guides me warmly across the lobby into the western side of the building. "This is the all-important Peace Garden."

It's beautiful. Like an indoor rain forest. Warm, tropical air with a humid touch. Plants, flowers and the cool trickle of a fishpond. I peer inside it and smile at the bright, colorful koi that swim about in the clear water.

"Aren't they lovely?" Dr. Gold says, kneeling gracefully down by the pond and tickling one large orange-and-white koi. "My little friends. They've been here as long as I have. I like to come and talk to them when I've had enough of insensitive businesspeople."

I stare at her, in awe. A room like this is perfect for someone like me. Someone who can get overwhelmed and overstimulated.

"We call it the Peace Garden"—she gets to her feet and strokes the leaf of a towering plant—"because we know how overwhelming the experience of Pomegranate will be for some. Some will need respite or preparation time."

I nod, slowly. Looking around the beautiful, tranquil room.

"I think I like it more than the restaurant," I murmur.

"Hey." She smiles at me, so kindly. "Me too."

I laugh.

I reluctantly leave the Peace Garden and follow Gregor and Dr. Gold to the elevator.

"The auditorium, cloakrooms, lockers and restrooms are all downstairs," she says matter-of-factly as we get inside and she presses the button for the second floor. "So I won't bore you with all that. In fact, we won't be on the second floor for long. It's marketing and HR. Boring grown-up stuff."

I laugh again. She isn't like other grown-ups. And I like that a lot.

The second floor is busy. People crowd around computer screens, talk into headsets and pass tablets around. There is a glass room at the end of the floor, where a large group of people are all seated around a table.

"They're launching a new campaign," Dr. Gold tells us. "They're all perfectionists and workaholics. We'd better not disturb the hive."

She makes a face as she says this, and I hear myself laugh again.

"Your floor next, huh?" she says to Gregor, nudging him gently in the ribs. He laughs too, and I notice him blushing slightly.

We reach the third floor. It's an open office full of cubicles, lots of people with furrowed brows in front of their desks.

I can see Gregor belonging on this floor. All the computing experts, the tech workers.

"I'll have to leave you here, Cora," Gregor says, slipping into one of the cubicles. "Can you manage without me?"

"Of course she can," scoffs Dr. Gold heartily, and I am thrilled. "Better just us girls anyway. You can come down and meet her for lunch. I'll take care of her."

"I know you will." Gregor smiles at us, with a really relaxed smile that I'm happy to see on his face.

"What's on the fourth floor?" I ask eagerly as we head up once again.

"Okay, I know I sound very flighty," she says sunnily. "But this is another one of my real favorites."

She nudges me in the same way she nudged Gregor and I laugh.

The doors open to reveal the quietest floor so far. It has actual rooms, rather than an open-plan office space like the previous two floors.

"These are our Waiting Rooms," she says in a soft and loving tone.

The doors are all numbered and closed. Each one painted a different, bright color.

"What are they for?" I ask her.

"They are the heart of everything we do here at Pomegranate," she tells me, pushing open the door closest to us. It's as red as a fire engine. I move inside and am hit with warmth and tranquility.

It's designed like a parlor. Or a beautiful hotel lobby. Soft armchairs and a coffee table with a china tea set. A large mirror on the wall. A tinkling, twinkling chandelier.

"Nice?"

She's genuinely asking me, gauging my reaction. The earlier feeling of importance swells up again inside me. I feel so grown-up. Appreciated. Respected.

"Very nice," I reply, irritated that I can't think of a better word. "Cozy."

That's not much better.

It seems to please her, though. She squeezes my arm.

"What are these rooms for?"

"Well, the clue isn't exactly in the name. They're meeting rooms."

"Meeting rooms?"

She meets my gaze and her face is full of serenity and gentleness. "Yes. Where people will come to meet the Grams."

I suddenly remember what Pomegranate is about. What it's for. I glance around the spacious and relaxing room once more. Trying to picture someone sitting in the soft pink, plush armchair.

Talking to a ghost.

I remember Gregor's explanation. That the Grams were virtual representations of people. Their brains, souls and personalities uploaded into a hologram.

"How do you do it?" I ask her.

She points up to the ceiling and my eyes follow her finger.

The ceiling is rigged with small but complicated-looking lights. At least, they look like lights. The kind used in the theater.

They are all pointing at the same spot, the second of the two armchairs.

"Those will cast the hologram," she explains gently. "So that the guest can sit with them. As if they're just having tea together."

My mind is a labyrinth of questions. I can't pick which one to ask.

"It's a lot, I know," she says softly. "I'm happy to answer any questions for you. The program can be quite frightening and overwhelming at first. But digital immortality is something we've all been talking about and aiming for since artificial intelligence was possible."

"Won't the holograms work out that they're dead?" I ask, staring at the little tea set.

"Ah, that's where my programming department does come in," she says triumphantly. Her eyes sparkle as she speaks. "We do our own fiddling and interference to make sure the Grams are calm and that, while they can adapt and observe, they won't question their reality. It relies on our guests too, though. They will be asked to sign a contract promising not to divulge any compromising information to the Grams. But most people will just want to talk. Talk about silly things, little things. Things they miss talking about with that person." I stare at the empty pink chair. I try to imagine what a Gram would look like. Act like. Sound like.

"You must come back again," Dr. Gold tells me, and it fills me with enough warmth to distract from the sudden strangeness of the room. "You can have a session with someone of your choice. And I'll have more time to answer any questions you think up in the meantime."

I gaze up at her. "Thank you, Dr. Gold."

"You are most welcome, Cora."

ALONE IN THE UNIVERSE

"My dad was *not* happy when he found out Gregor took me to Pomegranate."

Adrien and I are in his garden. Cerby is chasing a pigeon around the grass while the two of us sit in a patch of sunshine.

"What happened?" he asks me.

"Dunno," I reply. "They locked themselves in the car and yelled at each other for about twenty minutes. Then came back inside and didn't say a word for the rest of the evening."

Adrien snorts. "Well, my parents like to have long, screaming arguments in front of me at dinner. I wish they'd go to the car."

I eye him carefully. "What do they fight about?"

I can't imagine what there would be to fight about in his house. I glance over at the town house. Full of fancy ornaments and expensive art. Fresh food from the finest markets in London. Curtains with fabric from Paris, Mrs. Hawkins had told me. Someone paid to clean up after you. Cook your food, drive you around town.

What on earth is there to argue about?

"Me, mostly." Adrien sighs loftily.

"Why?"

"Dad wasn't keen on me being taught at home. Said it would ruin me."

"Ruin you?" I scoff. "What does that even mean?"

"He's very particular about seeming normal. Keeping up appearances."

I feel my smile slip. I stare at Adrien. Forcing myself to take in every detail of his face in order to read what's really going on. "Adrien, what did you mean last Saturday when you said I was like you?"

He finally looks up at me and says plainly, "We're both different. Our brains are different."

My blood chills and my fingers tic in anxiety. "What?"

"Well, they are," he says, shrugging. "You're autistic and I have ADHD."

I hate this feeling. When people know, and not because I've told them. I can tell when a teacher at school has been informed. People's behavior changes. The same way their behavior changes when they hear about Mum dying. Suddenly it's all the same sickly pity. The same patronizing voices.

"Who told you that?" I breathe.

"Your brother mentioned it to my dad. Why, is it a secret?"

"No," I say, bristling. "But it's none of your business."

I spot a flash of hurt in him, but he recovers quickly. "But it means we're kind of the same."

ADHD. I've heard of it, of course, but I've never met someone who had it.

"They're like cousins," he adds, placing his hands together like he's praying. "Our brains are from the same outer circle."

I blink. I've never considered that. Most of the information the doctor gave me after my diagnosis ended up as a pile of discarded homework.

"We're both different," he repeats. "And that's why we get on so well."

"Get on so well? You followed me!"

"And you knocked me to the ground!"

"Because you were following me!"

He lets out a boom of laughter. He flicks his hands in an excited way, like he's shaking off invisible raindrops.

"So, what's ADHD like?" I ask, a little dimly.

He catches me out immediately and fixes me with an "are you kidding" look. "What's being autistic like?"

"Fair enough," I mutter. I hate explaining myself. I won't make him do it either.

He smiles, satisfied.

"Well, I don't see what you dislike about Pomegranate,"

I tell him, changing the subject completely. "It's brilliant. Really cool."

"Oh, yeah?" His tone is sarcastic.

"Yes," I snap, shoving him lightly. "It was really great, and Dr. Gold was amazing."

"Oh, Sabrina?"

I'm weirdly envious that he knows more about her. "Yes. She's a genius."

"Why, because she's always so peppy?"

I roll my eyes. "Whatever. You wouldn't get it."

He laughs and rolls onto his back, staring up at the piercing blue sky. I do the same. Wondering for a second why this strange new friend allows me to forget about the horrors of school, Dad and Gregor's fighting, Zoe being thousands of miles away and in another time zone.

And Mum.

"Know what I like to imagine?" he asks quietly.

"What?"

"That right now, we're on the bottom of an ocean."

I twist my neck awkwardly to stare at him. "Come again?"

"Look." He points a finger up at one solitary little puff of a cloud in the sky. Its presence shows just how much space there is between us. Between the two of us on the grass and the sky. "We're at the bottom of an ocean, only one that isn't made of water. And the sky is the top of the ocean. The waves."

"Uh-huh."

"And just over the top of those waves is another bed of grass. Where two people are lying and pointing up at the top of their ocean."

I sputter for a second and then let out a laugh. A proper belly laugh, unlike anything I've laughed in ages. "What?"

"There could be a whole other world just over the top of the sky."

"Sure, Adrien. And how would you know that?"

"I don't." He grins. "But I would fly a plane up and find out."

"Into space?"

"Nah, just over the tops of the clouds."

"You can't fly a plane. No one is allowed to fly planes like they used to."

"I can. My uncle Max teaches me. He has a little plane of his own and he lets me take lessons."

"Seriously?"

"Yep. And when I get really good, I'm going to fly up over the top of the clouds and see what's there."

I've never been in an airplane. No one I know has. People aren't allowed to fly like they used to years ago. Even Zoe had to take a ship to get to Australia. If Adrien's uncle has a plane all to himself, he must be incredibly rich.

"What does flying feel like?" I whisper.

He lets out a huge breath, every inch of him smiling. "It feels . . . like being on the steepest, most exciting roller coaster. Except you're in complete control of it. You're in charge of the butterflies in your stomach."

"That sounds all right."

"It is."

I squint up at the bright sky. "So, who are the two people lying down above the waves, then?"

"Just two aliens like us."

I flinch. "I'm not an alien."

"We both kind of are."

"No," I say sternly. "I'm not."

Cerby bounds over and starts trying to lick Adrien, sending us both into delighted laughter. I feel the momentary flash of annoyance disappear and go back to wondering exactly what it must feel like to fly.

A GRAM

The more I stare at the clock on our classroom wall, the slower the hands move. I consciously remind myself not to look at it, desperately trying to keep my attention fixed on other things.

I stare down at my folder. A blank page where information about the Nazi invasion of Poland should be.

I look back to the clock.

I'm desperate for school to finish because Adrien and his dad are picking me up to go back to Pomegranate. We're going to have a light meal and then I get to meet one of the Grams. I'm ecstatic, so ecstatic that the day has moved more slowly than the snails Gregor used to steal from the yard and hide in his sock drawer.

"Cora?"

I turn at the sound of my name, hearing it being drawn out with a whiny, wheedling tone.

"Yes, Rebecca?"

Rebecca and her gang of friends are peering down at me, looking a little like meerkats. I didn't realize until Zoe moved how much I relied on her to smooth my way through school. She tells me, when I call her, all about her new friends.

I'm amazed at how many she's managed to get since arriving in a totally different hemisphere. She makes it sound so easy. Seamless.

I don't understand it at all.

"You're in our group."

Rebecca speaks slowly to me. As if we don't speak the same language. It's entirely possible that, in her mind, we don't. None of the other girls look thrilled about the fact that their leader is talking to me.

"Group?"

"For the project?"

"Oh." I finally get her meaning. History. We're supposed to work together. "Yes."

She lets out an exhale and then a short laugh, like a mum who is exasperated, and then fixes the most perfectly fake smile upon her face. "Do you want to just do your bits and then add them to ours when it's time?"

Group projects. Something I hate. I really am better at working alone. I used to be enthusiastic and excited about working with other people. But there's only so many times you can be laughed at, left out and ignored before you get the message.

"Sure," I tell Rebecca, nodding a little too heartily. "That sounds fine."

They all seem to let out little sighs of relief, glad that they don't have to tolerate me during their study session.

"Cool." Rebecca slides the worksheet toward me, snaps up her highlighter and sections off some pretty large chunks of the assignment. "There you go. If you can get this done by the deadline and just let me see it the night before? Thanks."

I hate myself a little for trying so hard to be nice. I'm about to tell her that of course I can do that, and I will, but she's already turned back around to keep chatting with the others.

I pull the worksheet toward me and gently slide it into my bag, not saying a word.

The bell rings and my glumness vanishes. Pomegranate. It's time.

I always find myself holding my breath when I rush out of the school building. The crowds, the lack of space, it gets too close to me. It's like breaking the surface when I finally reach the playground. I take in big gulps of air and spot the black Lexus parked right up by the gates.

"That's not your car."

I turn to see that Rebecca and Gemma are staring at the car as Magnus and Adrien get out of it. They haven't seen me yet, they've just been alerted by the throng of people exiting the school.

"That's my, um . . ."

What is Adrien exactly? A friend? He says so but it just seems so quick. It feels easy and natural, but I'm aware that the rules appear to have changed in recent years. Suddenly boys and girls can't be friends anymore. We all have to move in separate packs.

But Adrien doesn't care at all about the rules. "He's my friend."

I surprise myself when I say it. It just came out.

"He doesn't go here, though," Gemma says, as if the idea that we could be friends with kids from other schools is ludicrous.

"No, he's homeschooled," I explain.

Magnus is gesturing to Adrien's untucked shirt and saying something I can't hear, with a stern expression. Adrien is ignoring him. He suddenly looks up and spots me, and his face twists into a massive smile. He waves, making sure to do so as obviously and cartoonishly as possible.

I sigh and shake my head.

He resorts to doing the running man. Then some strange sort of tap dance.

Magnus shakes his head and ducks into the front seat of the car, slamming the door behind him.

Adrien then uses the school wall to pretend that he's walking down some invisible stairs. His lower half starts to disappear, and then his torso before he ducks and hides. I splutter out a laugh and then clap my hand over my mouth.

Gemma and Rebecca are looking at us both as if we are obnoxious.

I find that I don't really mind.

I saunter over to the wall, peering down at him while he pretends to be asleep.

"That was quite a show."

"Thank you," he replies, not opening his eyes. "I do six a week, plus matinees."

"Get up, I want to get going."

He grabs my wrist to haul himself up and smiles when we're face to face. I shake my head and pretend to be exasperated. He opens the back door of the car and I, a little self-consciously, slide in.

"Hi, Mr. Hawkins."

"Magnus, Cora, please," he says genially, without glancing up from his tablet.

"Move over!"

Adrien nudges me and gets into the car as well, shutting the door with a snicker. He takes my bag from me and throws it at his feet. I pinch him and he pinches me back.

"Are we ready?"

Magnus clicks his finger and the driver, Lloyd, sets off. I clear my throat nervously and look out my tinted window. I've never been on the other side of one of these before. People come right up to the car, completely oblivious to my face mere inches away. Staring up at them.

"Now, Cora." Magnus addresses me and my head

snaps around to look at him. "I'll brief you before we go in to meet the Gram, okay? It's still a prototype but it's worth doing."

"Okay," I say quickly.

"Just talk to them like you would anyone. Like you would a person in the hospital, for example. Now, if you were visiting a person in the hospital, you wouldn't talk to them about them being poorly, would you? You'd talk about nice things."

I think about Mum. About the drip in her arm. The way she swore at one of the nurses.

"Okay," I say quietly.

"As long as you don't break the reality," he goes on, swiping frantically on his tablet while he addresses me, "then it should be just fine."

"What happens if someone tells them they're a Gram?"

"They get super confused," Adrien answers for his dad. "Disoriented. None of them have worked out yet that they're not human, and if you tell them, they just get super upset."

"Which is why we don't do it," Magnus says firmly. "It's cruel. They feel, they have emotions. It just disturbs them. They're programmed to settle into their new reality. It's a huge violation of our terms and conditions to rid them of that."

"Understood," I say softly.

"Excellent. Now, touch. They are going to look incredibly real, Cora. You may want to touch them."

I don't interrupt him to tell him that I find most touch too intense.

"If you try, you won't feel a thing. They're a hologram, after all. They won't know that, though."

"So . . . I just have to play along."

I'm used to that. Most people aren't autistic. I have to play along all the time.

"Exactly right," Magnus says, beaming at me in the rearview mirror.

We drive a little longer and Magnus answers his phone to take a work call. I lean into Adrien and whisper, "So who am I meeting?"

He mimes zipping his mouth shut.

"Oh, come on," I fizz. "Tell!"

"She's some actress but I don't know her movies!"

Celebrities. I know that's another part of Pomegranate.

Celebrities who are still alive who provide their likeness and their digital soul so that members of the general public can "meet" them.

My fingertips tingle and I'm nervous and thrilled. Adrien seems less enthusiastic about it, but then he's probably so over Pomegranate by now.

The car parks outside the building and Magnus ends his call. I follow him inside, smiling tightly at the receptionist. She signs me in like before and nods at Magnus and Adrien.

"Are you ready?" Adrien asks me as we stand in the marble lobby.

"Yes," I say shakily. "Who is it?"

"It's Della Lacy," Magnus tells me as the three of us get into the elevator.

My jaw drops. She's in everything. Action movies, comedies, award-winning dramas. She started as a Harlem jazz singer and then went into fashion magazines, and then movies. I love her movies.

Mum loves her movies too. Loved her movies. We would go to the independent movie theater in town to watch her films. Mum would take her shoes off and stare up at Della in wonder.

So would I. When I wasn't watching Mum.

"So, Cora." Magnus steps out of the elevator. We're by the Waiting Rooms. "Take a moment when you see her. Sit down and get settled and then we'll wake her up, all right? Only once you're ready. Get your nerves and initial reactions out of the way and then signal."

I don't know what to expect, or how to signal, but I nod quickly. Magnus seems satisfied. He gives Adrien a gentle shove. "My son will go in with you. He's a pro at this now."

Adrien exhales wearily but gives me a wan smile and nods reassuringly.

I take a deep breath and, after a nod of permission from Magnus, I step inside the Waiting Room.

She's there. In the room.

She sits in the pink armchair, facing us, with her long legs crossed at the ankle. She's completely frozen, like a photograph.

But she looks so real. Her bright eyes, her beautiful hair. She looks just as she does on the movie screen. Bright nail polish. Pearls.

I sit, a little unsteadily, opposite her and suddenly have no idea what I'm going to say. I stare at her. At the Gram. She looks like a friend you've been speaking to over a video call who has suddenly frozen on-screen. Her clothes are pressed and clean.

She seems so physically, unequivocally human.

"Ready?" Adrien murmurs.

I feel a catch in my throat, but I hastily nod, never taking my eyes from her.

Adrien lifts his arm as he sits next to me and, as if by magic, she comes to life. Someone somewhere is watching, they must be, but I don't question it right now.

I'm too amazed.

"Oh." She laughs musically and looks straight at me. "Sorry. Lost my train of thought there."

"That's okay," I whisper. "How . . . how are you?"

I'm not good at making small talk with human beings, let alone holograms, but she lights up at the question.

"Never better, my love," she says, smiling. "Thank you. How are you?"

"I'm good," I say truthfully. "Long day at school."

The Gram's face morphs into the most devastatingly beautiful expression of empathy. She leans forward a little and for the first time in a long time, I'm enjoying the eye contact. I can see flecks of gold in her brown eyes. Everything about how she looks is smooth and perfectly toned. She's like a fine painting. Only real. So real, I keep having to stop myself from saying so out loud.

"I always hated school," she says, like it's a beautiful secret.

I let out a rush of air and laugh once. "Really?"

"Oh, yes," she says, her voice silvery. "You'll look back and laugh one day, my angel."

I stare into the most human eyes I've ever seen and feel a tear drop onto my cheek. Her eyes widen in compassion and she reaches out to wipe it from my face. While I cannot feel her touch at all, while I cannot let her know that there is no substance to her gesture, it's the most connected I've ever felt to another person.

SOCIAL LESSONS

"It's quite something, isn't it?"

I'm sitting in the beautiful, tranquil Peace Garden on the ground floor of the Pomegranate building. I'm looking down into the cool, clear pond at the koi. Dr. Gold has quietly sat down next to me without any fuss.

"Yes," I answer her. "It's . . . incredible."

"But a lot to take in, I know." She drops some food into the pond for the fish. "It's such a dream come true, this place. And I had to fight. I mean, I'm a scientist. Not a businesswoman. But the amount of pitch meetings I had to fight in."

I don't know what to say but I really want to please her. "It's amazing."

"Thank you, Cora," she says gently. "Thank you. I'm glad you understand what we're trying to do here."

"I mean, Della is still alive," I say quickly. "But I would probably never get to meet her if it weren't for this place."

"Yes."

"It's so incredible. So, if that's what it's like to meet a celebrity, I can only imagine . . ."

"What it's like to see your loved one again," she finishes for me. "I know."

"It's"—I try quickly to say something profound—"like a miracle."

She smiles down at me. "That's a lovely thing to say."

"Was it your idea? The Waiting Rooms?"

"Yes," she responds. "I . . . well . . . I lost my mother. And that was the hardest thing I've ever been through. I've been the only STEM graduate in a lab full of boys, I've fought my whole career to be taken seriously. But losing her was the hardest thing I've ever had to fight."

I stare up at her, trembling. "My mum died too. A year ago."

She meets my stare and her eyes shine with almost-tears. "Really?"

"Yeah!"

She laughs sadly and squeezes my hand. "Then you know."

I nod, frantically. I do know!

*

I'm completely burned out and overstimulated in the car journey home, so I just let my head rest against the tinted window and listen to Adrien as he rambles on about flying.

"God, it's really got to you, hasn't it?"

I come back into the moment. "Huh?"

"That place. The Gram. They've got to you."

"In a good way," I tell him. "The best way."

He scoffs. "It's all a trick."

"Adrien." Magnus actually turns around in his seat to scold his son. "Be quiet."

"It's not a trick," I whisper sharply. "I wasn't being tricked. I know she was a hologram."

"It. It was a hologram."

"She."

"You really think AI can accurately re-create a human being?"

"After that?" I jerk my thumb in the direction of the facility that's fading into the distance as we drive back to my house. "Yes."

His social battery is clearly as worn out as mine so neither of us speaks as the car zooms through the quiet streets. I put my headphones on. I let my favorite songs wrap around me like old friends. The music acts as a soothing balm after a lot of stimulation. I scroll through my phone, pulling up Della's social media. I'm amazed and delighted to see that the images she has uploaded look exactly like the Gram. Just as beautiful, just as alive.

I shake my head softly at the mastery of what Dr. Gold has done.

When we arrive at my house, Magnus walks me to the front door.

"One moment, Cora." He addresses me before I go inside. "I'm so pleased you liked Pomegranate."

"I loved it," I admit.

"That's excellent to hear. Now, I think Greg has mentioned this to you. I'm afraid I've badgered him quite a bit about it."

"You want to interview me for the facility?"

He smiles, the laughter lines around his eyes becoming more defined. "Well, yes. I appreciate your candor."

"My dad is dead set against it right now, Mr. Hawkins."

"Magnus. And I thought I might have a word with him about that."

"And the answer would still be no."

Magnus almost topples backward off our front doorstep as the door flies open and Dad makes this pronouncement.

"Dad." I speak through gritted teeth. "It's an amazing place. You won't believe—"

"Get inside, Cora."

Magnus is smiling at Dad, having regained his composure. "Lovely home you have." He looks the outside of our house over with the same expression Rebecca and her friends wear when they see me every Monday morning. "I don't get to come to this part of London as much as I'd like."

"You should," Dad says coolly. "It's where the real

Londoners are. Not the weekday visitors from Surrey. Or yacht fanatics."

The smile on Mr. Hawkins's face slips. "Yes. How charming."

They shake hands, firmly, while I slide by Dad to get inside the house. As I turn, I catch sight of Adrien leaning against the car. Looking very serious.

He isn't looking at me, though. He's looking at Magnus.

And I can't name the expression. But it looks strange on his usually cheerful face.

*

I'm at school and exhausted. I stayed up late trying to finish my part of the history group project. I kept getting distracted from my work as I remembered Della and Pomegranate. I watched clips of her movies and marveled at how remarkable the accuracy was.

I don't regret it.

"Is that it?"

Rebecca falls into the seat next to me and nods her head at the folder in front of me.

"Yup," I say, rubbing my eyes and sliding it toward her. "Here you go."

She flips through everything I've done, speedily and with quite a lot of disinterest for someone who asked me to do half the work.

"It looks fine," she says eventually, sliding it back. She digs in her designer bag and pulls out a transparent folder. "Can you tidy up Gemma's parts?"

I look over at Gemma. She's texting on her phone and talking to Sian. I slide her homework for the group project out of the folder and wince. It's poorly written, underwritten and just plain bad.

It will take a lot to rework. "To be honest, I'll probably have to rewrite this."

I expect Rebecca to take the paper back but instead she nods and says, "Cool, that works."

Before I can say anything else, Mr. Ramsey and Ms. Mabuse arrive. I shakily pull Gemma's work and mine toward me. I only have tonight to work on it and I'm supposed to be having dinner at Adrien's house. Recently, I've been so overtired and overstimulated that homework has been almost impossible. I've taken to doing most of it in the restroom at lunchtime.

Mr. Ramsey is joking and laughing with some of the boys as Ms. Mabuse makes her way over.

"Everything okay, Cora?"

I quickly shove the two homework folders into my backpack. "Yep."

"You sure?" she asks, eyeing Gemma and Rebecca.

"Oh, yeah," I say quickly. "All good here, Ms. Mabuse."

I can tell that she doesn't want to drop it but Mr. Ramsey begins the lesson and so she is forced to.

I clutch my bag, knowing that the entire history project is inside and now up to me.

"Right." Ms. Mabuse addresses the class, holding up a stack of papers. "I need you all to take one of these by the end of today, because I know you don't check your emails."

Titters of acknowledgment ripple across the room. I gingerly reach out and accept one when she offers.

A dance. A school dance.

I love music. It sets everything in me alive. Every hair stands on end. I feel like there's a box in my heart; a secret, hidden part of myself. I keep so many things locked inside that box so that no one else will ever see. And when I listen to music, alone in my room with my giant headphones on, the box flies open and all the colors spill out and somehow merge with the music. I love the feeling. All my masking and my reservations leave, and the hidden parts of my soul come out.

I can't do that in front of other people. I've tried school dances before. Girls stand on one side of the room, boys on the other, and instead of sharing the sensation of the music, people play silly social games. Whispers, looks and pointing.

I used to ignore all the others and dance on my own. Until Zoe begged me not to. The dances meant a lot to her, socially. There was always a boy she wanted to notice her. And my dancing would reflect badly on her, I think.

So, I won't be going to this dance.

"Are you going to go?" Rebecca asks me, nodding toward the pile of information sheets.

"Oh." I put mine in my bag but shake my head. "I don't think so."

"I think that's probably for the best," she says, while Gemma cackles and the others splutter under their breath. They turn away from me, shoulders shaking.

I stare toward the front of the class and think about going to Knightsbridge and getting far away from here.

*

The smell of cooking hits me the moment I enter Adrien's house and my stomach rumbles loudly in response. I skipped lunch to do the history project in the restroom and my stomach has been complaining ever since. However, upon smelling seafood, tomato sauce, garlic and spices, it growls in complete desperation.

"You're here!"

Adrien's mum, whose name I've learned is Ria, pokes her head out of the kitchen at the end of the hall. She's kicked off her heels but is still immaculately dressed. A shiny leather skirt that pulls in tightly at the knee, a white silk blouse and a polka-dot apron. Her icy-blond hair and red lipstick look too perfect for someone who has just been cooking dinner.

Bella suddenly appears next to her, oven gloves on and carrying a large pot of pasta.

She actually looks like someone who has been cooking.

"Go get seated in the dining room, sweet peas, we're almost ready to serve up!" Ria calls out cheerfully.

Bella sighs and then adds, "It'll be ten minutes."

Adrien grabs my bookbag from me and drops it into the cupboard under the stairs. He then leads the way into an extremely fancy dining room. Not that I'm used to comparing dining rooms, we don't have one at our house. The only one I've seen before is the one on the Clue board. And this one doesn't look anything like that.

A black marble table with six large leather chairs all around it. A bowl of lemons sits right in the center along with two long candlesticks. Adrien drags one of the white leather chairs along the varnished floorboards and sits down. I hesitate. Knowing not to sit at either head of the table but feeling strangely shy about sitting next to him.

"You can sit," he says merrily.

I settle for the chair opposite him.

"Another crummy day?" he asks, using his hands to beat out music on the marble table. I watch how speedily they move and how the energy just seems to flow through him. He can't sit still. Not when there's music—he's the same in the car. I sometimes want to ask him if he feels the same exhilaration as I do when listening. Is music medicine for him, like it is for me?

"Suppose."

"What happened?"

"Well, what exactly was it that made you realize school wasn't for you?" I ask him directly. Choosing to stare right at him.

His hands steady a little and he considers the question. "I was never on everyone else's speed."

That's not quite what I expected. "What?"

"I was either going way faster than everyone else or I was finding it hard to even concentrate. I mean, if I find something boring my brain sort of shuts down."

He doesn't strike me as someone who gets bored easily. But he does, from the time we've hung around together, seem to have a social battery.

Like me. He's up and loud and excited until it runs out and then he needs to be alone.

"Teachers kept saying that I wasn't trying or applying myself. That I was being lazy. And I didn't know how to explain to them that sometimes my mind literally switches gears if it's not engaged. I was good at maths and history but not spelling. But because I was really good at those other subjects, they said I wasn't working hard enough in spelling."

It's eerily familiar. If you're extremely good at one subject, some teachers don't understand how you can be really bad at another.

"Plus, the other kids found me weird," he adds quietly, taking up his percussion again. "So Mum let me leave."

Before I can say anything else, Ria bursts into the room carrying an enormous and ornate bowl.

"Salad!" she cries, as if that's the most exciting thing in the world. "Bella's taken over the main course, but salad is my specialty."

Cerby has trotted into the dining room behind her, his nose moving quickly as he tries to work out if the mysterious food in the fancy bowl is something he can eat. After Ria ceremoniously places it on the table, Adrien fishes out a crouton and tosses it to his dog, who catches it snappily.

"Oh, behave," laughs Ria, returning to the kitchen.

Cerby bounces along after her.

"I just don't know how to navigate school without Zoe," I say honestly, the acoustics in the room letting my voice reverberate a little. "She just got people. Understood them. She knew how to make friends in three seconds."

Adrien frowns. "We became friends in three seconds."

I exhale. "Okay, but that wasn't normal. It wasn't the normal way. Zoe makes friends in three seconds the *normal* way. By asking all the right questions and saying all the right things."

"Why do you care so much about being normal?" Adrien asks, exasperated. He grabs a piece of lettuce from the salad and bites into it.

"Why do you not care enough?" I snap back, snatching

a piece of tomato. "Do you want to be left out your entire life? Because I don't."

"I just don't care anymore," he says freely. "As soon as I gave up caring, everything got easier."

"Well, it's different for boys anyway," I sigh.

We sit in an uncomfortable silence for a moment. Unusual for us. Sometimes we don't speak because we're both out of battery, but this isn't like that.

"I'm just hungry," I eventually mumble, bridging the gap. "I didn't get to eat lunch."

He nods understandingly. "Why not?"

"I was in the restroom doing our group history project."

He blinks. "In the restroom?"

"Yeah."

"Why not the library?"

"Our school doesn't have a library. And we're not allowed in the classrooms or corridors during breaks. So I have to do homework in the restroom."

"But you said it's a group project."

"Well, yeah." I wave away the question. "The girls I'm paired up with, one of them couldn't do her part properly so now I'm doing it. It's due tomorrow so I had to do it during lunch."

"What? Why?"

"What do you mean, why? It's due tomorrow."

"Why the hell are you doing other people's work?"

"It's not like that." I shush him angrily, glancing at the open door. "We're getting graded as a group."

"Then everyone should be doing their fair share."

I shush him again as I hear voices drawing nearer and footsteps in the hall. Bella and Adrien's mum enter, one carrying a huge bowl of linguine with mussels, garlic, chili, tomato and squid and the other a plate of fresh, warm baguettes.

"Here we are," Ria says happily, arranging the table and beaming at the two of us. "Dig in."

She and Bella sit down with us and I tentatively place the fancy linen napkin in my lap. Adrien loads up his plate with pasta and mussels and I do the same, the smell completely glorious and sending all the difficulties of the day away to some forgotten place.

"I think it's just so great that you're both fast friends," Ria chirrups as she pours herself a drink. "Treasure that. It's something you can only do when you're young. I miss that, you know." She smiles widely at us. "Being able to have a new best friend in just a few short hours. It's such a gift."

I've never met a grown-up who has ever been able to really sell adulthood to me.

"Not long left until the summer holidays." Adrien's mum charges ahead with the dinner conversation while her son and I shovel food into our mouths. "I really mean it, Cora. You must come over whenever you like." Dad and Gregor will still work all the way through the summer holidays so it's not a bad idea. Better than being dropped off in Hyde Park with a tenner, to be collected eight hours later.

"That would be nice, Mrs. Hawkins."

"We usually summer in France but Adrien's father is so bogged down with work, we're stuck in London this year."

I don't really know what to say to that so I settle for polite formality. "Thank you for dinner, Mrs. Hawkins, it's really delicious."

"Oh, of course," she gasps delightedly. "No thank-you needed; I'm just so thrilled Adrien has a chum."

"Pomegranate was also really impressive," I tell her.

She glances up and her face seems to freeze for a moment before blossoming into a fuller smile. "I'm glad you liked it. Did my husband show you around?"

"No, but Dr. Gold did."

"Ah, yes." Ria's smile dims a little. "The mastermind behind the whole thing."

"She's so inspiring," I say, after swallowing a large clump of linguine and tomato.

"Yes," Ria says softly. "Quite the career woman."

I suddenly hear Cerby leap to his feet and run into the room. He runs to Adrien's side and whimpers slightly. The sound of the front door opening can be heard.

"Bella!" Ria whispers sharply.

Bella quickly clears her plate and leaves the room, heading to the kitchen. I watch, bewildered.

Magnus Hawkins enters the room and smiles when he sees me.

"Cora. Hello there."

"Hello, Mr. Hawkins."

"You're home early," Ria says, taking a big sip of her drink, her ring clinking against the crystal glass.

"Wanted to be home for Italian night," Magnus says, kissing her briefly on top of her head. He frowns at Cerby before sitting at the head of the table. Bella appears, apron on, with a plate for Magnus. He accepts it and Bella leaves the room again.

I'm not sure I understand why.

"What did you learn today?" Magnus asks, and it's clear he's talking to Adrien.

Adrien stabs a mussel with his fork. "We went to the rose garden in Hyde Park to talk about botany."

Magnus's cutlery clatters onto his plate and he fixes Ria with a stern glare.

"It was a lovely day for it," she says defensively. "Cora, what are you learning about?"

I gulp. "Well, right now we're doing a project on World War II."

"You see?" Magnus gestures to me but looks at Adrien. "That's useful. That's important. Why can't I come home to dinner and hear you telling me all about that?"

"Dad, if you don't know the basics of World War II by now, I don't know what to tell you," Adrien says dryly.

"That's not funny. You should be studying history. Economics. Science."

"Botany is a type of science," Adrien rebuts. "It's biology."

"Physics. You should be learning about physics."

"Flying is the only physics I need," Adrien says, winking at me. I smile, despite myself. "Academia is too dull. My brain needs live action, gotta keep things moving."

"You think it's all a game," Magnus says quietly, wrapping strings of linguine around his fork with perfect precision. "You think this malarkey will be fun and cute when you're older? It won't."

"It's not fun and cute now, it's just who I am," Adrien says firmly, dabbing his chin with his napkin.

I can tell this is a regular argument. One that has been rehearsed and rehashed to perfection. Mum and Gregor used to have them. Sometimes Mum and me.

"It's just who you are?"

"Magnus." Mrs. Hawkins speaks quietly, squeezing her glass tightly. "Please."

"We have, each and every day, a choice about who we are," Magnus goes on, ignoring Ria. "Don't let a condition define you, son."

"Okay, Dad," Adrien says sarcastically. "I won't let my brain—you know, the most important, central organ we all have—I won't let that define me. I'll be defined by my pancreas instead."

Magnus pushes his chair back and the sound of it is sudden and grating. Adrien leaps to his feet and whistles sharply. He walks quickly from the room and Cerby follows instantly.

"Fine," Magnus calls after him. "Take that mangy animal out and for God's sake, don't bring it back."

"Magnus!"

I stare down at my lap. I'm mortified. I eventually peer out at Ria. She is staring into her drink, saying nothing and looking at no one. Mr. Hawkins eats his food, his expression blank.

I quietly get up and leave, knowing where Adrien will have gone.

I find him in the garden, throwing sticks for Cerby. "Your dad must have had a rubbish day at work."

"No," he says, not looking at me. "He's always like that."

"My mum had a stressful job," I tell him, sitting down on the grass. "She used up all her energy during the day being nice to colleagues. So she was super angry and exhausted when it was all over. She'd snap and lose it a lot."

"Grown-ups aren't supposed to lose it," Adrien says coldly, throwing the stick with such force that Cerby flinches before diving after it. "They're supposed to have it together."

"I know," I say softly.

He exhales and falls down next to me. "He wants to change me."

I don't know what to say to that. We watch Cerby gnaw and maul the stick and we say nothing for a while.

"Wanna know something about being autistic?" I tell him.

He looks at me. "Definitely."

I feel a tug in my stomach as he says it. He's the only person I've ever told this to, and the only one who has ever shown any positive interest.

"I have really heightened senses," I say carefully. "Some places in London . . . they're like sensory feasts. Like London Bridge? I can smell all the bread in Borough Market long before I can see it. And the smell of the river. In Brixton, I get off the train and I can smell the fish and the pineapple. Certain places have sensory trademarks, and autism lets me feel them all."

"Wow." He looks around us. "What about here?"

"Knightsbridge?"

"Yeah."

I hesitate. "Well, to be honest . . . it doesn't really have one. It's just a lot of gasoline."

He nods. "That sounds about right. Not much alive around here. Just money."

"But your house smells great." I nudge him. "Especially tonight."

He smiles. "Yeah. When Dad's not home, it's great." I don't know what to say to make him feel better. So I just sit with him.

"You shouldn't do other people's work in the group project," he eventually says.

"It would be more difficult if I didn't," I tell him flatly. We sit in more silence. An ambulance siren wails in the distance. Most people can't tell the difference in sirens, but I can.

"Our school's having a dance," I hear myself say. "You're lucky you don't have to go to things like that."

"Why don't you want to go?" he asks, looking at me. "I've seen you with your headphones on, you love music. You jam out when you don't know I'm looking."

"Don't be embarrassing," I say, pushing him. He pretends to topple over and I laugh.

"You don't want to go?" he presses.

"I would go," I admit, "if none of the other kids were there."

I wait for him to mock me but, as I've come to expect, he doesn't.

"I get so mad at myself sometimes," I say under my breath. "I try to be like everyone else but the things they all find so easy, I find so hard."

"Well." Adrien pats his leg and Cerby comes running to him. "I think you're looking at all the wrong things."

I turn to glare at him. "Why do you want to be friends

with me? Why did you decide that? Because you don't have any of your own?"

I'm trying to provoke him, but he ignores it, scratching Cerby's ears. "Because we're the same. I've seen a lot of kids over the years. My parents have forced me on a lot of playdates. Gone on holiday with other families and their kids who are my age. My time in school. My time in summer camps. Being forced to go to other people's houses where they're all too dull or too mean. I look at them and I know we're the same age, same background, same everything. But I just know. I know we're not a good fit."

He pulls some blades of grass out of the ground and lays them gently and reverently on Cerby's head, between his ears.

"But when I saw you here, on my birthday, looking all angry . . . I knew. I just knew. We were the same. We were a good fit."

The sound of the siren fades away as we sit side by side in the garden. Not needing to say anything else.

POISONED FRUIT

"Gemma, Rebecca and Cora? Can you stay behind, please?"

Rebecca glares daggers at me as Mr. Ramsey makes the humiliating request in front of the whole class. We all sheepishly nod, and I sit and wrack my brain over what he could possibly be mad about as the lesson drags on. Ms. Mabuse isn't in today and I'm feeling the loss.

When the bell finally rings, we wait for the others to run off before we approach his desk.

"Now, I'm not angry," he says carefully, reaching into his drawer to pull out a folder.

The folder. The one I put the whole history assignment into.

"It's clear from your project that someone has done a great deal of work and someone else has done the absolute bare minimum."

I frown. I don't understand.

I watch him pull out a sheet of paper and feel my skin sizzle with horror. It's Gemma's work. The original sheet that Rebecca asked me to redo. I last saw it in the restroom as I frantically tried to rework it. I was certain I had trashed it when I was finally done. But then, I had been in a rush near the end of lunch and I had been so hungry . . .

I feel a piercing shot of pain in my head as I realize that I must have trashed the piece of work I had struggled so hard to get perfect.

"Now, I just want to stress that the entire point of teamwork and a group project is to learn to collaborate and delegate. So . . . this is disappointing. Because the majority of the work is sound."

"It's my fault, Sir," Rebecca says on an exhale, looking demurely at the carpet. "I take responsibility."

Mr. Ramsey frowns but nods sagely. "Okay, Becca."

"I said I would redo Cora's parts. Then I just got so tired and forgot to do it."

My head shoots up and I gape at her. "What?"

"Cora did her best, I think. But it just wasn't up to snuff." She gestures to Gemma's barely legible addition, the one she is lying about and saying I wrote. "I was going to rework it, when Cora refused, but I just got so exhausted."

She lets out a fragile little sigh and her face crumples. It's an incredible performance. I'm slightly in awe but also horrified.

Mr. Ramsey puts the project back in its folder and shakes his head. "Cora . . . I must say, I'm more than disappointed. This is exactly what I was talking about the other week when I said you needed to learn to work with others."

I can't speak. My ankles are hurting because I'm pushing down into the floor so much. My knees feel like they might buckle. Every part of me is hot and indignant. I can hear Adrien's voice in my head, demanding that I stand up for myself. That I correct Mr. Ramsey. Tell the truth.

But no sound comes out. I don't say another word. I take the demerit. Silently.

*

I'm still silent at dinner, staring at my fish cakes while Gregor and Dad talk about soccer.

"You're quiet," Gregor finally remarks, eyeing me. "Everything okay?"

I nod slowly. I can feel them glancing at each other.

"I got an email from the school," Dad says, in a forced tone of cheer. "There's a dance, then, eh?"

I shrug. I can't talk. I can't make the effort, I just . . . cannot.

"You've been pretty isolated this year, pet," Dad persists gently. "I think that would be fun for you. You and Zoe used to love those things."

Silence.

"Maybe Adrien would be allowed to go," Gregor volunteers. "He's the life of the party anyway."

"Yeah," Dad agrees with a reluctant laugh. "How about that, then, Cora?"

I don't look at either one of them. I get to my feet and clear my plate before going up to bed. I fall onto the mattress and feel every sore, unfair prod of the day like a bruise on my skin. I can hear them talking downstairs, I can hear the worry from all the way up here.

But I still say nothing.

*

"She did *what*?"

Adrien is at my house. Dad got Gregor to call and invite him over. It's a new day since Rebecca threw me to the wolves but I still feel aches and pains from the completely casual betrayal.

"She's sneaky," I say. "I couldn't speak, I was so stunned."

"You've got to get back at her."

"No." We're sitting on the sidewalk outside the house eating Popsicles. Lloyd is napping in the front of the Lexus and Cerby is chasing butterflies. "No point."

"God, I'm so angry," mutters Adrien. "We should toilet-paper her house."

I have to laugh. "Or we could just let it go."

"I'm not letting it go."

"Stop being a bad influence." I nudge him with my foot.

"Bad influence? I'm a good influence. I'm the good influence you need in order to stick up for yourself, Cora."

"You've been out of school too long, you don't get the politics of the classroom," I say, laughing.

Eating Popsicles with Adrien, on a hot summer afternoon, makes the horrid parts of school seem less important.

"Hey, I've got a plan for us today," he says suddenly, slurping the last of his Popsicle and heading toward the car. Lloyd snaps to driver mode instantly, putting on his dark glasses and sitting up straight in his seat.

"What are we doing?"

A few weeks ago, I was always wary of Adrien. Wondering what his intentions could be and why he was so different from other kids our age. Now, when he says something predictably unpredictable, I'm excited. It's a game. We're going to have fun somewhere.

Lloyd takes us to Holborn and drops us off, refusing to tell me what Adrien has planned for today's excursion.

"Why can you never be surprised?" Adrien needles as we walk through the streets toward wherever he's taking me.

"I like to know exactly what to expect from my day," I grumble, looking longingly back at the car. "For all I know, you're taking us for a tour of the sewers."

Adrien stops dead in his tracks. "How did you know?"

I glare at him. "That is not funny, Adrien Hawkins. You are not taking us to the sewers of London."

"Cora, you would be hard-pressed to find someone who loves sewage more than me."

"Will you shut up?" I'm desperately trying not to laugh because if I laugh, then he wins.

"Mum's got me reading Victor Hugo and, wow, does that guy love sewer systems."

"Where are we going?"

"I mean, you must kind of love them as well, seeing as you brought them up."

"I'm ignoring you now."

"Were you secretly hoping that's where we're going? I can change the plan. Do you know there's a whole secret river under London? It's called the Tyburn."

"How do you remember all these useless facts?"

"Now, now. There are no useless facts, Cora."

I pretend that I'm about to kick him and he laughs and darts out of the way. I'm about to actually kick him when we turn the corner and I stop completely and stare up in wonder.

"Ta-dah!" he bellows, crouching low and throwing his arms out in presentation.

It's the British Museum.

I feel complete elation and joy but then it quickly turns

to fear and anxiety. I'm suddenly aware of all the sensory elements around me and I start to feel a little overwhelmed.

"What's wrong?" Adrien asks, his smile fading.

"Nothing."

He can't understand. He's the best person I know, but he's grown up with money. He feels comfortable walking into every room. He's never had to explain to the teacher why he can't make a school outing because it's been scheduled before payday or because Dad couldn't change shifts. He's never been twenty pence short on the shopping and had to decide what to put back, a whole queue of people behind you watching and waiting.

And tutting.

"It looks so grand," I tell him quietly. Grand and frightening.

"Let's go!"

He tugs me along and I stare up in fright as the building looms over us, growing bigger and bigger as we join the winding queue to get in.

"I don't have any money," I tell him, whispering low so that the family in front don't hear.

"It's free," he replies, matching my hushed tone. "Well, donation. But I'll donate."

I'm nervous when it's our turn to enter the building. Adrien taps his card against a machine after selecting a donation price, and it beeps. We go in, it's that easy.

I don't have a bank account yet. Not that much could go in it.

"By yourselves, kids?"

A guard is looking at us with suspicion. He angles his body so that he's blocking the entrance to the gift shop on the left.

"Yes, we're here to look at all the stolen things," says Adrien.

I roll my eyes. He gets feisty when adults try to pull rank on him.

"Well, pay special attention to the signs that say no touching and no climbing," the man says slowly. Like we're toddlers.

"Cora." Adrien looks at me with mock seriousness. "Don't climb on the Egyptian sarcophagus."

"Okay, Adrien. And don't you go writing on the Rosetta Stone."

The guard swears softly but walks away from us, leaving the entrance to the museum open and inviting. Adrien sets off confidently, familiarly. Like he's very used to coming here.

I follow, steadily but not as stridently.

Upon entering the main atrium of the building, I am staggered. The light-filled space seems vast enough to shelter its own small population. I could never have dreamed there could be such a wide-open indoor space like this anywhere in London. Like a giant birdcage, housing many colorful species of time.

It's a kingdom.

"Good, isn't it?" Adrien asks softly.

I feel tearful. Fragile. Like the huge building has exposed every part of me that has ever felt less than.

I know I could have walked in here at any time in my life. There are no actual gates keeping me out, not really. I have as much right as anyone else to wander in and spend afternoons looking at objects and exhibits.

But the invisible barriers. They're hard to acknowledge and impossible to walk through. They've kept me out of so many places and away from so many people.

"If I weren't going to be a pilot," Adrien says as we make our way up the stairs to the first gallery of our visit, "I'd be a museum curator."

He's always so sure of everything. "Why?"

"Well, it's a good job for people like us," he says breezily. "We can turn our special interests into a job."

"Special interests."

"Things we're, like, obsessively passionate about. Like for me, it's Alan Turing."

The name is familiar, but I don't want Adrien to know I don't know exactly who that is.

"He was a codebreaker and a megagenius," Adrien tells me anyway. No judgment, just excitement. "He worked at this place called Bletchley Park during World War II. He helped decode Nazi messages."

Suddenly I remember where I have heard the name before. There was a portrait of him in the office where I was diagnosed. Along with Albert Einstein, Beethoven and a bunch of other historical figures that doctors now believe were undiagnosed neurodivergent people.

"They think he was autistic," I say quietly.

I half expect Adrien to frown and shake his head. Refute the theory. Instead he nods enthusiastically. "Yes!"

"I mean"—I shrug and speak rapidly—"we'll never know, and some people obviously don't think we can be geniuses."

"Rubbish people."

"But a lot of people at the office I was in think he was. Didn't something happen to him?" I ask, looking over the edge of the pearly staircase at the tiny people milling about below.

"Yeah." Adrien's excitement fades a little and his voice grows slightly sad. "He died. Poison. After they branded him a criminal for being who he was. For being gay."

The conversation feels too raw.

"He was one of the early founders of the technology we have today," Adrien adds bitterly. "And they beat him down."

We stand side by side in dense silence for a moment. "What about Pomegranate?"

Adrien glances at me when I ask the question. "What about Pomegranate?"

"Couldn't they bring him back?"

"No," Adrien says firmly. Defiantly. "No, they couldn't."

"Why not?"

"Because whatever they do only works in the slightest because they study people who are currently alive. And even then, they get it wrong."

"No, they don't."

"Yes. They do. And besides, Alan Turing is what the Turing Test is named after. It's how you measure artificial intelligence. It would be too creepy."

"You don't want to meet him?"

"But it wouldn't be him!" Adrien insists, frustration leaking into his voice. "I want to meet *him*. The real him. The human him. Not some digital copy. And I never will. But that's the sad, horrible thing about life. You have to do everything you want as soon as you can and there are some things you're just never meant to have. And places like Pomegranate just promise you a watered-down lie."

"You're so harsh on Pomegranate."

"Not harsh enough, believe me."

The silence falls again, and I wonder how we got here.

How he can find a place that I think is so miraculous, so horrible. How he can be so disdainful about it—doesn't he see what a lifeline it could be? How much it could help those who have lost someone?

"Come on," he says warmly, nudging me and jerking his head in the direction of the gallery. "Let's go look at some old stolen stuff."

I smile and nod, and we hop up the final steps and onto the gallery floor.

It's a great day. We have fun, as usual.

Mostly because neither one of us brings up Pomegranate again.

Adrien sometimes talks and acts as if he has a hundred tabs open in his brain. Like he's giving a speech and watching a movie and reading a book all at the same time. But then, when it's something really important, he focuses so hard and so fully. Gives it the most undivided attention I've ever seen.

It really is quite remarkable.

I'm still thinking about it as we arrive, an hour or so later, back in Knightsbridge. Adrien is about to hop out of the car but then sees me staring out the window lost in thought.

"What's wrong?" he asks.

"Nothing," I answer. I look around the street, one of the richest parts of London. "You're just really lucky, Adrien."

"Yeah, I know."

I don't know why I feel so sad after such an amazing day. Maybe because it's over.

"Hey, guess what?" he suddenly says. "I told Mum

about that dance thing and she said she could lend you all the clothes and makeup you want. Jewelry too."

My head snaps around and I stare at him. "Excuse me?"

"To borrow. For that school thing."

All the overwhelming feelings of the day flare up into something I can't name. "I don't need charity, Adrien."

"What?" He frowns in confusion. "No, it's not like that."

"You don't need to feel sorry for me. You don't need to meddle. I don't want to go to that stupid thing and if I do go, I'm capable of doing everything myself."

"I know you are." He waves away my irritation. "Just thought it might be nice."

"Yeah, nice for the kid with the dead mum and no money."

I don't know where on earth that came from, but it came out. He stares at me, staggered. Even Lloyd, with his back to us, draws in a short breath.

"Sorry," I mumble, pushing my hair behind my ears and opening the car door. "I'm going to get a bus home. Sorry. See you later, thanks for today. Sorry."

I stumble out of the car and make my way toward Harrods in the hope of finding some public transport. Lloyd starts the car and slowly trails alongside me while Adrien leans out of the window.

"Let us give you a lift."

"I'm fine." I'm angry at myself. I don't know where this is all coming from.

"You're burning out."

"What?" I snap.

He holds up his hands as a sign of peace. "No, I get it too. It's okay. It's normal. For us, I mean. It's normal for us."

"I'm fine, I just want to go home."

"I didn't mean to sound all patronizing about the dance thing," he says hurriedly. "It was just something Mum offered."

I feel a stinging stab in my side. "Tell her thanks but I'm fine."

"Hey, Cora?"

"What?"

He catches my fingers. Not my hand, just the fingers. Like he knows the feeling of having my hand grasped would be too much right now. He squeezes them so lightly.

"You're my best friend, Cora."

It quiets the strange anger in me. And feels like a release. Like a dam breaking apart to allow all the water out. I take a moment to breathe. I can't say anything back to him, but I squeeze lightly in response. I stand on the sidewalk for what feels like an eternity. Adrien never lets go and doesn't say a word. Finally, when I feel ready, I get back into the car.

Lloyd drives me home and Adrien still holds my fingers

while I focus on my breathing. I can't even begin to explain what happened. Where all the emotion, the pain, the anger suddenly bubbled up from. Why I felt like I couldn't mask a second longer.

I've always found spending long periods of time with people difficult. No matter how much I love them. My battery runs out and I can't function on empty.

And I know, since Mum died, I haven't been the easiest to be around. The grief is like a headache when it rains. It arrives unannounced and it hurts. And it makes me say things that I normally wouldn't.

Adrien has so many people around him who love him and want to keep him safe at all times. He's never alone.

I've always been alone.

THEATER

"What's going on?" I ask Gregor as we enter Pomegranate.

A security guard is chewing gum with his mouth open and checking everyone's passes before they file downstairs into the lower ground level. He checks mine, then Gregor's and allows us through.

"Staff meeting," Gregor informs me. "Thought you'd want to see."

I do.

The lower ground floor of the Pomegranate building is a large staff room and then some kind of theater. It has tiered seating for the audience to look down at a small stage with a screen and a podium.

Gregor and I sit in the middle of the auditorium while other Pomegranate technicians, the marketing team and additional members of the staff saunter in, all talking among themselves. When everyone is starting to sit, the lights dim, and the stage area is lit with harsh, professional lights. Dr. Gold and Mr. Hawkins step onto the podium and everyone applauds.

I glance around me and quickly applaud as well, wondering what's about to happen. Everyone seems to be teeming with excitement, whispering to each other and shoving their phones away to pay close attention.

"Thank you for that welcome, everybody," Mr. Hawkins says, gesturing for people to hush as he speaks into the podium microphone. "Thank you. We thought we should do this before we get into all the work that's going to be undertaken this summer. I appreciate all the hard work you've done so far."

He clears his throat, stiff and formal. His words are clipped and clinical. He glances at Dr. Gold, who is smiling serenely at the whole room.

"I know those of you who have been in technical and design have heard a lot of this already, but our newer team members should really be exposed to exactly what it is that we're trying to do here."

I lean forward a little as he speaks.

"Pomegranate," he says importantly, "is going to change the world."

There is a smattering of applause at this, some assured and enthusiastic. Some just because other people are clapping.

Dr. Gold nods imperceptibly at Mr. Hawkins and then steps up to the microphone, beaming proudly at her staff.

The energy in the room instantly changes.

"I know some of you have had long nights in the design process with me and will be tired of my spiel, but stick with me one more time, I'll cut down my gushing about how incredible you all are."

People laugh and I think I'm missing an inside joke.

But then, I often feel like that.

"What keeps me going when the press says what we're doing is overly ambitious?" she asks the room. "What motivates me when people say that science and tech have never gone this far? How do I carry on after all those evenings when we have to start over?"

She splays her hands open and inhales deeply.

"The fact that Pomegranate is going to let people live forever."

Sudden loud and rapturous applause. It makes me jump.

"I'm going to put a stop to people's agony. Their loss, their grief, their what-ifs. I'm going to keep families together forever, the way they should be."

She blinks against the bright lights that are focused on the stage and I realize she probably cannot see the audience very well.

"Who here has lost somebody close to them?" she calls out.

I watch everyone raise an arm into the air. I do as well. I look to Gregor and nudge him when I notice his arm is down. He rolls his eyes but reluctantly echoes the gesture. Dr. Gold nods slowly and raises her own hand. I know she can't really make me out in the dark, but I nod too. We're the same. We've been through the same horrible mess. We've both crawled out of the same hole.

I can be as strong as her one day.

"I don't want people to ever have to say goodbye to their loved ones."

She lets those words spread across the rows of seating like a blast of warmth after feeling nothing but cold. They hit me hard and unfreeze something in me.

"I know those of you in marketing and outreach haven't actually seen the product yet," Mr. Hawkins interjects. "Apart from lovely Noma at reception, who is designed specifically for the facility, some of you haven't yet met a functioning Gram."

I blink in astonishment. Then turn to stare at Gregor. He gives me a knowing smile and a small nod. I fall back in my chair and shake my head once, in disbelief.

She wasn't human. Noma is a Gram.

"So, for those of you who have yet to see one of Pomegranate's incredible creations, here you go."

People murmur and shift in their seats as Dr. Gold signals to the lighting desk at the back of the auditorium.

In a flicker, a frozen Gram appears on the stage. Some people gasp, others make noises of delight. It's a Gram of Dr. Gold.

"I wouldn't be much of a leader if I didn't experiment on myself first," she says laughingly, putting her hands up.

I laugh. Gregor doesn't.

"Now we have to be ready," Mr. Hawkins says firmly, "for what the press and the usual rabble are going to say. The perpetually offended are going to say this is unethical, that if Grams are intelligent and sentient then they should have rights and freedoms. It's such a boring argument, so be prepared for it. These Grams are digital pieces of people's souls. But they are not flesh and bone. You cannot hurt or maim them. They cannot leave their surroundings and take over the world, or whatever other clichéd horror stories we'll hear."

Dr. Gold clicks her fingers and the Gram awakens.

It jerks briefly upon seeing its new environment and then glances at the real Dr. Gold and Adrien's father.

"Can you tell everyone your name?" the real Dr. Gold asks, gazing fondly at her digital double.

"Dr. Sabrina Gold," the Gram says, every little detail identical.

"Occupation?"

"Head of the Golden Department at Pomegranate."

"And what is Pomegranate?"

"It's an institute for preserving life and allowing people to live forever, digitally."

"How?"

"Through holograms, informally known as Grams."

"Are you a Gram?" Mr. Hawkins asks the question and the room seems to collectively hold its breath.

"No," says the Gram, arching an eyebrow and looking bemused. "I'm not. But I create them."

The real Dr. Gold nods approvingly and clicks her fingers again. The Gram freezes and, after Dr. Gold signals to the lighting desk, it disappears altogether.

"I can promise," Dr. Gold tells the room, "that our Grams will not question the nature of their reality. I have designed them that way. I have given them digital blind spots. My own Gram doesn't recognize me because I built her that way. I reassemble people exactly as they are and then I remove the odd piece here or there so that they can function smoothly and calmly in their new ecosystem. Your colleagues in this room who have bags under their eyes have made sure of this. They have put in the work and the result is outstanding. Hence why they're trying so hard to stay awake."

A rumble of laughter.

"You can also see the resemblance is uncanny. Identical. It's the real deal. These are not cyborgs or androids that need battery charging and could potentially turn on us. They are us! Digital versions. People will see digital recreations of themselves or their loved ones, and they will be astounded. They will rejoice. And they will keep coming back to us, they will tell their friends to come to us. And, slowly but surely, we will change the world."

She smooths an invisible crease in her dress and smiles brightly out at us.

"Are you up for this phenomenal challenge?"

I rush out a breath and nod as the whole room gets to its feet to applaud her. I can't see over the people in front of me, cannot see Dr. Gold, but I clap all the louder.

DANCE

"You would be such an asset to this facility."

I smile up at Dr. Gold as she says it. I was having dinner in the restaurant at Pomegranate, waiting for Gregor to finish upstairs, when Dr. Gold found me. Now she sits across from me as I eat dessert.

"Dad really doesn't want me to be interviewed," I tell her, taking another bite of apple pie. "I don't know why but he's pretty firm about it."

"I think all this can be a little daunting for some people," Dr. Gold says warmly, looking around at the ornate surroundings. "Maybe if he came down and saw that we're not lizard people, he might change his mind. He doesn't mind your brother working here? Gregor does such a great job for the team."

"It's good money," I say sheepishly. "We're not the most well-off so I think Dad overlooks my brother being here."

"Hey, don't be ashamed of that," Dr. Gold says compassionately. "My family had no money when I was growing up. It was horrid. I used to be embarrassed at having to wear the same clothes over and over again at university. But I was smart. And I worked hard. That's way more important."

She gives me a knowing smile and, if I weren't chewing a mouthful of pie, I would return it. She always knows what to say to make me feel at ease.

Adrien wants to be a pilot when he grows up. I want to be Dr. Gold.

"I wish my mum were alive to see all this," she says quietly. Then she sighs. I want to make her smile again but don't know how to.

"I think she'd be really proud of you," I finally tell her.

She looks up and gives another dazzling smile. "Oh, Cora, thank you. That's nice to hear. You know, it doesn't matter how old you get, you never stop needing your parents in some way."

She dabs lightly at her eye with the tip of her finger. "That's why this place will be so good for people," she adds, smiling up at the chandeliers. "So many people walk around the world with so much anger and pain.

"Lots of lost orphans. If I could give all those people something to hold on to, I think the world would really change. Grief is like an open wound and our society doesn't know how to heal it properly. But I know."

I think about how I exploded at Adrien. Was it grief?

Was I one of those sad, angry people she means?

"So, if I let Pomegranate interview me," I say carefully, "I would really be helping the facility?"

"Not just Pomegranate," she says reverently. "You'd be helping everyone. When we open up to the world, and everyone starts allowing their selves to be uploaded as a digital double, we'll need to understand neurodivergent people fully. Right now, we just don't have enough research. You'd be helping us perfect the intricacies and specifics of people's autistic loved ones. Helping us re-create them just right, so their families can have peace. It would be the most unbelievably selfless act, Cora."

I look at my fragmented reflection in the dainty silver fork that I'm holding and wonder what it would feel like to be admired and praised by people like Dr. Gold and Mr. Hawkins. For helping make Pomegranate something really special.

"I'll talk to Dad again," I promise her. And she smiles.

Suddenly, we hear raised voices and commotion from the reception lobby. Dr. Gold frowns in concern and gets to her feet, moving swiftly but cautiously toward the noise. I follow, apple pie forgotten.

"You can't use my face!" a woman screams.

Dr. Gold is standing in the doorway while I peer around her. I gasp as I see what looks like Noma standing in the lobby, hair unwashed and eyes a little bloodshot. But the real Noma is also at her reception desk, looking bewildered and astonished.

"Noma." Dr. Gold moves to the Gram version and unplugs something behind the desk. The receptionist vanishes and we're left with a very agitated, but very human, double. "We've talked all this through."

"I didn't agree to this," the woman snarls, pushing her hair out of her eyes and pointing shakily at the desk. "I did not agree to him using my image and my frigging brain to be a creepy clone servant! He made me sign that thing, but I didn't know what I was signing."

"Noma, please let's discuss this," Dr. Gold says caringly. "I can go through the contract with you and we can decide how to move forward."

The woman's frantic eyes land on me. "Don't sign anything," she says, staring at me with such force, I immediately look away. "Whatever you do, don't sign anything away to this place."

She then storms out, pushing two technicians returning from break out of her way as she does. I look up at Dr. Gold, who is watching the real Noma go with an expression of sadness and disappointment.

"She was one of our first interns," she tells me quietly. "Was totally on board in the beginning. I don't know what's changed."

She squeezes my shoulder and then moves back to the

reception desk to plug in whatever it was she disabled a few moments ago.

The Gram version of Noma reappears. She blinks, taking a moment to familiarize herself once again. And then smiles at me, eerily identical to the woman who just left in hysterics.

"Welcome to Pomegranate." She beams, her voice sunny and upbeat. Not at all how the real one was a minute earlier. "I'm Noma, how can I help you?"

*

After days of changing my mind over and over again, the night of the dance is here and I'm going. Dad and Gregor have given up asking me about it and are just prepared to go with whatever I decide come seven o'clock. I'm wearing tattered jeans and my one nice top and have turned an old ribbon into a choker. A brush through the hair and one of Gregor's charcoal pencils has doubled as some eyeliner right on the edges of my eyes.

I put on my nice sandals and head downstairs. Dad and Gregor were whispering but they shut up as I reach the bottom step.

"Are we going?" Gregor asks nervously. I nod.

"Now, you call your brother the minute you want to leave," Dad shouts as Gregor and I make our way to the car. "Even if that's five minutes after he's dropped you off."

"Okay, Dad," I shout back, shutting the front door behind me.

It's a short but tense drive to the school. Gregor parks outside the entrance. People are filing in. Lights are flashing and music is pounding.

"Cora?"

"Yeah?"

He shuts off the engine and stares at the steering wheel. "I just want you to know, I think you're really brave."

I look up at him. "Why?"

"You're going in there by yourself. You do everything by yourself. I just think you're really brave."

I don't know what to say.

"I had a hard time at school," Gregor continues. "Being nerdy, being awkward. But I know how much harder it is for you."

I roll my eyes. "Please don't feel sorry for me, Gregor. I don't care what people think."

And for the first time in a long time, I almost believe myself when I say it.

"It's not too late for me to go and get Adrien," Gregor jokes, finally looking at me.

I smile. I ignore the urge to beg him to do just that. "I'll be fine. I'll go in, enjoy the music, eat the snacks and hide in the restroom if I get overwhelmed."

He laughs but I'm not kidding.

I can feel him watching me as I head toward the school entrance. I know I have no friends in there. I know I'll get looks. But sometimes I get so anxious about things like this, I miss out on experiences altogether. And I sit at home in my room, safe from whatever it is I'm afraid of.

But full of regret.

If I hate it terribly, I'll leave. And at least I will have tried.

I take a moment upon entering the assembly hall that's been turned into a dance to adapt to my surroundings. I let my senses get used to the new levels. Louder, brighter, busier.

People in my grade are already in their clusters, I notice upon walking into the room. The boys on one side, the girls on the other. The dance floor is still empty, but the DJ doesn't let that destroy his buzz as he puts on another track. A few teachers clutching bottled water are dotted around the hall.

"Cora?"

I turn to see Rebecca and Gemma. They're pretending to withhold giggles like they're in church. Way overdone, I get their point: they're surprised to see me here.

"What's up?" I say. "Need any more work done? Or are

you ready to go to Mr. Ramsey and explain what actually happened?"

Gemma goes as white as the paper cups people are drinking their fizzy drinks out of, but Rebecca purses her lips and takes a step forward.

"You can't prove anything, freak. Sorry to tell you."

"Well, I can, though," I hear myself saying, taking a step forward as well. "Because while Mr. Ramsey might have the intellect of a gnat or, you know, the two of *you* put together—Ms. Mabuse is smart. And she knows all our handwriting because she does so much of the grading. So, it won't take her a long time to figure out what actually happened."

Now Gemma looks petrified, staring at her leader with real fear. Rebecca pushes away from her terrified deputy and storms off, casting one glare back over her shoulder as she does.

I turn to Gemma and plaster on a fake smile. "Have a wonderful night, Gemma."

I spin around, sniggering, and feel a whole lot better. Then I notice something. Someone. At the bottom of the stairs. He's dancing with complete abandon, absolutely uncaring about all the kids and teachers now staring at him. In a black tuxedo and a white silk opera scarf.

Adrien.

I can hear myself laughing because it's just so absurd.

Seeing him here, in my school, dressed to the nines. Boys with badly gelled hair and untucked shirts stare at him, perplexed, as he spins around like a top. The girls look on in fascination and bewilderment. The teachers are utterly baffled.

I'm still laughing.

The music is pulsing and upbeat, and Adrien moves freely and fluidly to every note. While definitely a bit jerky, I'm astonished at how good he actually is.

Maybe it's the complete lack of self-consciousness? Totally abandoned to the music.

I'm *still* laughing. People must think I'm out of my mind. Laughing loudly enough for Adrien to look up and spot me. He grins widely and waves. I can feel people watching me now, probably wondering who on earth this person is and how we know each other.

As the music continues to blast, Adrien tosses an invisible lasso.

"No!" I yell over the speakers, laughing. "Absolutely not!"

He ignores me and tosses it again. I'm laughing so hard, I think I might combust. I don't feel my usual fear and terror at being stared at. I actually realize that I don't care if they're all finding me strange.

They don't have what we have. And I feel sorry for them. I start to hop toward my friend. As if I've been caught by the invisible rope he's cast over. He laughs loudly, thrilled I'm joining in his game. When I reach him, we clasp hands and run in place, getting out all our energy.

He follows my lead, copying the corny dance moves I've learned from Dad and Gregor over the years. The whole hall is watching but I don't care.

I just don't care.

Hip bumps. The swim. The twist. He sits on the floor, I sit behind him, and we pretend to row invisible oars on an imaginary boat, in time to the music.

We finally start our own conga, Adrien leading and me behind. As we move around the large hall, I finally get a good look at the other kids. I spot Susan, Fateha and Maria, all girls in my class. They're at the edge of the dance floor, looking on in wonder. As I grip Adrien's waist, trying to keep up with his fast and free movements, I feel another pair of hands grip me. I glance back to see that Maria has joined our conga. Susan and Fateha hesitate but then click into place behind her.

Five quickly becomes ten, which then becomes almost everyone in the room. Adrien leads us around the room in time to the loud, thrilling music and I scream with laughter. With happiness.

This is the lightest I've felt in my whole life. I'm fitting in. I'm belonging. Nothing's forced, nothing is faked.

I'm having fun. And the strange realization of that, alongside the feeling, makes me giddy. When the song ends, everyone is hooting and laughing. All the awkward barriers have been broken down and we all stand together in the middle of the floor, alive and loud.

I wrap my arms around Adrien from behind and squeeze. "You're the best!"

"Nah," he calls over his shoulder. "I just love to boogie."

SPECTRUMS AND SPECIMENS

"How long until they work out I don't go here and kick me out?"

I laugh at Adrien's question. We're sitting on the steps outside the school, at the front entrance. We're drinking pop out of the white paper cups and sharing a bag of candy.

"You got everyone to actually start enjoying themselves. Maybe they'll overlook the gate-crashing."

"This school doesn't seem too terrible," he remarks, glancing back at the brutalist building. "Nicer than the private schools Dad had me in."

"What's so bad about private school?" I ask, hogging the bag of candy.

"They didn't really like me. What with my ADHD."

"I thought private schools were meant to have all this extra support."

"They call it support. It's actually tons of handwriting

workshops, meetings where they tell you why you're not fitting in right. Counselors telling you to change your entire brain and try harder."

He doesn't sound bitter about it. He's smiling. But there's an edge.

"It felt"—he stretches his legs out—"like I was failing at a job I didn't want. But instead of firing me, they kept hauling me into the office and telling me why I should be fired."

It sounds familiar.

"I like me," he says quietly. "Not all day every day, but most of the day. I like my brain. I like my pace."

I look at him. And smile.

"I've never really said that before," he chuckles.

"I like you too," I say, nudging him. "Even when you're incredibly annoying."

"Hey, I've just bought you a ton of street cred in this place."

"Oh, sure."

We sit in the warm evening air and look up at the London sky. I've never seen the stars. Not in all their glory. Not enough to see all the constellations together.

Sometimes, one peeks through. One single star. I can see it now. It's one of those clearer evenings.

I stare up at it. Bright enough to shine through the polluted air.

"I want to do an interview for Dr. Gold."

I blurt it out, still staring at the solitary star in the night sky. I feel him freeze next to me. I turn to look at him.

"What's it like?" I ask. "Being interviewed?"

He says nothing. Looking up at the star himself.

"I know you've done it," I persevere. "I know you've been interviewed there. So . . . what's it like?"

"It's nothing special," he says lightly. "Just scientists. It's tiring. And some of the questions are really pointless. Not clever."

"Scientists have to be clever," I point out.

"They're super smart, but no one can be clever about everything."

I'm taken aback. But I know he's right. Gregor is the smartest person I know but he can't change lightbulbs. Meanwhile, Dad has always struggled with reading. Yet he has the best memory of anyone I've ever met.

People's minds are all so different. All capable of different things.

"I want to help people," I push on. "If they need to study someone like me, then I'm happy to do it. If it will help people."

"Help people? You think Pomegranate wants to help people?"

His scoffing makes me turn a little red. "Well. Yes."

"Cora, they want to make money. If they can charge people to come and talk to their dead grandmother, or something that looks, sounds and acts like their dead grandmother, then they're going to do it. It's not charity. It's a business."

I look away, embarrassed. "I don't agree."

"You don't know my dad."

"You don't know what it's like to lose someone. Too soon. With so many things you haven't said. Lots of bad threads that haven't been tied up. You don't know."

He looks up at me and I hate the pity in his face. "Don't," I say crossly. "Not from you. Don't. It's not about that, it's not about her. I just think you don't understand why people need this."

He nods slowly. "Okay."

My defenses settle back down and I glance up at the star once more. I listen to the distant thump of the music and the excited shrieks of the other children.

"Do you know why I hate the word 'normal'?"

I don't answer him. I don't ask him why. I'm afraid of what he is going to say, because he's suddenly so much more serious. And Adrien is never really serious.

"It's because all I ever wanted for years was to be normal," he says, looking up at the night sky and the one bright star. "I could never tell you what 'normal' is, I'm not sure anyone can. But I learned really quickly that whatever it is, I don't have it. And not in a fun, kooky way. Sometimes I felt like everyone else knew the language of the world and I was just trying to get by with a few odd phrases. From a book that's, like, twenty years old."

I close my eyes. It's too familiar. Too honest.

"And if I ever try to tell them that," he says to me, and I'm not exactly sure who "they" are, "they'll just say, 'Oh, everyone feels like that sometimes, Adrien. Everyone feels a bit different.' "

He scoffs, bitterly.

"But they have no idea," I say softly. "They don't realize that unless you hide who you are, it's constant."

"Yes," Adrien says, looking at me intently, still far too serious. "And you know what? I worked out how to fix it. Forget it all. Forget all the nonsense. All the ridiculous rules that don't make sense and the rubbish one-size-fits-all way they want us to be, forget it all. I stopped caring what other people thought, stopped caring about trying to fit and I was free."

"Easy for you to say," I murmur despondently.

"No, it isn't."

I look back at the school building. And wonder what it would be like to walk away from everyone else's opinions of me.

"Cora, the reason they always tell me, 'Oh, your ADHD doesn't define you,' is because it makes them feel better about it. Because the minute you find out what makes you different, the minute you love it and accept it and say you wouldn't change who you are, that's when you become dangerous."

"Dangerous? Did you say dangerous?"

"Yes. People who like themselves are very dangerous."

"You're very full of big ideas tonight," I say teasingly.

I slip one foot out of my shoe and press it into the stone. Enjoying the sensation.

"You should like yourself more."

I laugh, but I'm a little unnerved. "Shut up."

He smiles, reluctantly. I think the subject is dropped and am about to suggest going back inside when he adds, "There's a reason why we're different. You and me. Why we're made this way. And it's for us to decide. It's none of their business."

I look from Adrien to the star and then back to him. "Okay, Adrien. Duly noted."

It starts to rain. So lightly. He moves to get up, but I touch his elbow. "Can we sit in the rain for a bit?"

He watches me but doesn't ask why. "Sure. Sure, Cora."

We sit under the gentle drops of water and I exhale. "Thank you for coming tonight. For . . . what you did."

He reaches over and hooks his pinkie finger around mine.

And that's all that's needed.

*

"You look happy."

I smile at Dad upon arriving home. Gregor picked me up at the very end of the night and was astonished when

I asked if he could drop Adrien off in Knightsbridge. We spent the car ride reliving the entire evening and laughing as we remembered the initial looks of shock on everyone's faces. Gregor seemed too stunned to say a thing.

"It was a great night," I tell Dad, joining him in front of the television.

He beams at me, looking up at Gregor as if to check if he's seeing what Dad is seeing. "Cora, that's . . . that is really great. I'm so pleased for you."

I feel good and guilty at the same time. Glad that Dad seems so thrilled about me having a fun evening, but guilty that he's clearly been worrying about me.

"Adrien was there."

Dad's eyebrows shoot up when I say it. "Oh."

"He gate-crashed. But it was great."

Dad splays his hands out in front of him. "Well, I hate to say it, but that boy has been a good friend to you."

"Why do you hate to say it?"

"Dad's loath to admit anyone rich can be decent," Gregor says from the doorway.

"Behave," Dad mutters, but he doesn't deny it.

In that instant I decide to take advantage of the good feeling in the room.

"Dad, I want to let Dr. Gold at Pomegranate interview me."

Both Dad and Gregor are stunned into silence by my sudden statement. Gregor hovers in the doorway and then rushes into the living room, sitting down in front of me. He looks hopeful and amazed. I can feel Dad's anger radiating next to me.

"I know you don't want me to," I say steadily. "And I don't really understand why. But I think if you met Dr. Gold, you would see it's a good idea."

"Cora." Dad sounds weary and I wish I hadn't brought it up. "I'm saying no. I'm sorry if that seems confusing or unfair, but I'm saying no. You'll understand when you're older."

"I'm nearly thirteen," I say bitterly. "I can understand whatever it is, Dad."

He smiles at me sadly. "Let's not ruin your lovely night."

I roll my eyes but accept the olive branch. I watch Gregor, who is clearly biting his lip about the whole thing.

I can't imagine what it is they're scared to tell me.

POCKETS

It must be the hottest day of the year.

Adrien and I are leaving Hyde Park with Cerby. I'm going to miss the glorious floral scents as we return to Adrien's neighborhood, but the weather is so wonderful I don't really mind.

The streets are quiet, apart from some fancy cars racing around and around. It's not uncommon, this area is a playground for the rich and they like to show off their fast toys.

But they make the most terrible noise.

"I'm guessing your dad wasn't thrilled about you wanting to interview at Pomegranate," Adrien says, handing Cerby's leash to me so I can walk him for a spell.

"Nope," I confirm. "Don't think he'll change his mind about it either."

"Well, good," Adrien chuckles. "I don't know why you like the place so much. Gives me the creeps."

"You saw that Gram. It's incredible."

"It's smoke and mirrors. And the mirrors have a bunch of creepy scientists behind them, all watching you."

"It's a person! A digital person, Adrien. It's amazing. Of course I'm interested in that."

"What about real people? Aren't they much more interesting? There's nothing I would hate more than to be one of those creepy Grams."

"You're so irritating."

He laughs. We keep walking, approaching the main part of the road before we head toward his square. I can hear engines revving in the distance, so annoying and obnoxiously loud.

"Would you want them to make a Gram of you?" Adrien asks me suddenly, standing on the road with his toes touching the sidewalk. He blinks at me in the fierce sunshine, waiting for my answer. I spot a woman on the other side of the road, Adrien almost exactly halfway between her and me. She's wearing designer sunglasses and has the most beautiful hijab on. Bright fabric, made of silk.

"I don't know," I say honestly. "Wouldn't be much good now. I'm only twelve. But when I'm older, I'd make one. So my family could still see me."

He steps backward onto the empty road, smiling nonchalantly.

"I don't think they'd be able to get you just right, Cora."

"Oh, now, what does that mean?" I ask despairingly. "What, I'm too weird for Pomegranate?"

"Yeah," he laughs. "But that's a great thing!"

I laugh. Cerby barks.

And then it all happens so quickly.

A car, a sports car, lurches around the corner, not taking a moment to slow down. It screeches and tries to swerve, but it's too late. It collides.

It hits him. Like a flicker. So fast, it happens in a breath. And I have no breath to scream.

Adrien doesn't just hit the road, he flies. I let out a silent scream and my vision goes for a moment.

I'm by his side but I don't remember running to him. The car backs up and speeds off, the two men inside it arguing so loudly I can hear them as they fade away.

"Adrien," I manage, clasping his hand.

Cerby is whining and Adrien is still blinking up at me, fighting against the sun like before.

"I'm calling an ambulance!"

The beautiful woman in the hijab is next to me, on the phone. She grips my arm tightly, her face a flush of horror. "Keep him talking, baby, and don't move him," she tells me quickly before standing and shouting for help over the phone.

A sleepy part of my brain doesn't understand why we would need an ambulance. They're for terrible accidents. This is like something from a nightmare, it can't be real.

We'll be all right.

"Adrien, she's calling now. It's going to be fine."

His eyes are fixed on mine and I don't dare look away.

I smile and squeeze his hand.

He blinks so slowly. So mechanically.

"Those stupid racers," I laugh nervously, a tear slipping free and falling onto the piping-hot road. "They're such idiots. But you'll be fine."

"Cora," he rasps. "My mum. I need my mum."

I glance over my shoulder at the woman. She's rushing back over to us.

"Yes, he's conscious," she tells someone on the phone. "But it's really bad, he went flying. They must have been going twice the speed limit."

"Just stay awake," I tell him. "And your mum will meet us at the hospital. Okay?"

He closes his eyes for a moment. "Don't go anywhere, Cora."

"I'm not going anywhere," I say hoarsely. "Okay? Not anywhere. I'm right here, Adrien. I'll ride with you to the hospital and get you whatever you want from the vending machines when we're there."

"Cora?"

His eyes are closed now, and his voice is so quiet.

"Yes?"

"I'm scared."

"Nothing to be scared of, Adrien," I assure him, stroking his hand. "Just a bump. All is going to be okay."

I can hear sirens in the distance. An ambulance.

His eyes finally open and stare up at the sky. The bluest sky. I follow his gaze.

"That big ocean, remember?" I say shakily. "We're just looking up at the top of our ocean. You just keep looking at the surface. You're going up there someday. In your own plane. So just keep looking. Keep looking, Adrien."

He's still staring up at the top of our blue ocean when his eyes soften and his hand falls from mine.

*

"Cora?"

I hear my name being distantly called for the third time. I glance up. My eyes are blurry, but I make out Dr. Gold. I'm sitting in some hospital room, alone, and Dr. Gold is here.

"I came with Adrien's father from work," she says, answering the unasked question.

"Oh."

"Cora." Her face crumples. "I'm so sorry."

I leap off the chair I'm sitting in and start to pace. I hate the "sorry." I hate the silence and the space and the embarrassment of this.

"He's going to be okay," I say stiffly. "They're going to do that electric shock thing to him."

"Cora, where are your family?"

"Gregor and Dad are coming." I called them. They were

at home and said they'd come straight here. To the hospital. "But he's going to be fine. CPR. Electricity. They'll do it."

Dr. Gold kneels down beside me and pushes my hair back from my face, her expression too painful for me to look at.

"Sweetie, he's in a bad way."

"No," I bark. "He's just gone for a bit. Just for a bit. But they'll bring him back."

"My love, he was unconscious on arrival. That car . . . it hit him too hard."

I bellow. She holds me. Really tight. I can smell pomegranate as I scream into her crisp white shirt.

At some point, Dad and Gregor come barreling into the room. I'm transferred from Dr. Gold to Dad without preamble. Gregor grabs my face with both of his hands.

"Are you hurt?" he cries, over my sobs.

"I don't care!" I scream.

"We need to get her home now," Dad snaps to Gregor. He starts carrying me like I'm four years old again. I'm wailing like a toddler. I can't help it, there's so much poison in me. Dark, metallic fear and I need it out.

I need all the hurt out.

I can make out Dr. Gold as I'm carried away. She looks so sad. So afraid for me. I don't look away from her as I'm hauled off. I hold on to her in my line of sight until the elevator doors close.

As the elevator goes down, something falls from my

pocket. The key. The golden key to Adrien's garden. He gave it to me, told me to come to the garden whenever I needed to.

"I need to give this back to him," I tell Gregor when he watches me bend down to pick it up.

"Who?"

"Adrien," I snarl. "I was just borrowing it. I need to give it back to him."

"I'll give it to Magnus," Gregor says gravely. "Okay?"

"No, give it to Adrien," I demand. "It's his key. His garden. Give it to Adrien. And someone needs to tell him that Cerby is okay."

But I don't hand over the key. I cling on to it. I won't let anyone but Adrien take it from me.

"Cora," Dad whispers. "Pet. Please. He's not here."

I kick out ferociously and Dad wobbles, needing Gregor to steady him and then pick me up. Like I'm a baby.

I don't remember the walk to the car. Or falling out of consciousness.

I don't remember anything else.

AWAKE

Wakes are like a really sad party.

I hated Mum's. Hated having to worry about appearances and small talk. Hated watching the coffin being brought out.

"Cora?"

I turn to see Magnus. He looks awful. This thought must show on my face because he nods and runs a hand through his slightly disheveled hair.

"Thank you for coming," he says in a low voice. "Not an easy thing to do, I know."

"It's okay, Mr. Hawkins," I say quietly.

"You really mean the world to him."

I don't know what to say to that. I watch him smile wanly and then move over to join the doctors out in the corridor, all of whom race to shake his hand. Vigorously.

I move farther into the room. It's all wires and machines. He looks like he's sleeping.

But not dead.

"Are you his sister?"

The nurse enters the room and speaks gently, watching me while she attaches another wire.

"No," I say, my voice dry and scratchy. "I'm his best friend."

"Oh," she says tenderly. "Then I'll bet he'd really like to hear your voice."

I move closer to the hospital bed. I can feel the brightness of the fluorescent lights in the backs of my eyes. "He can hear me?"

"We think so. It really can help to talk to them. Wherever they are, they'll want to hear you."

"Is he somewhere else, then?"

"In a way. We're doing everything we can to make him comfortable, help him breathe. He's still in there. He's not gone away."

"Adrien," I say, too quietly for anyone else to hear. "Where did you go?"

Coma. I didn't know the word before. The doctor explained that it is like a sleeping spell. One that they are trying to find the counter-curse for. He was soft and gentle with me.

"My name's Grace," the nurse says calmly. "I'll be taking good care of him, don't worry."

I nod. "My mum was a nurse."

I can feel her hesitate before saying, "Really?"

"Yeah. Before she got sick."

Grace makes a soft noise and reaches over to squeeze my wrist.

"Adrien's going to be fine," I say resolutely. "His brain is different. It's special. He's not like everyone else. He's going to make it."

"That's the spirit," she replies sincerely. "Good girl."

I back out of the room and spot them. The man who must be Adrien's uncle Max and Ria Hawkins. Their blond heads bowed together in the corner.

I move over to them, like I'm sleepwalking. "Can I get you anything, Mrs. Hawkins?"

She looks at me as if she's never seen me before and then says, "Oh, no, thank you. Thank you, Cora. I'm fine."

She looks the furthest thing from fine. I don't understand, on a day like today, why we all have to pretend.

I spot Dr. Gold sitting alone across the room. I move toward her. When she spots me, she smiles kindly and pats the empty seat next to her. I gladly take it.

"How're you holding up?" she asks.

"Enough."

"Good."

We sit in silence for a moment.

"Cora, would you walk with me? I have something I want to tell you."

I'm grateful for any distraction and I've run out of small talk, so I agree. We leave the hospital without telling anyone and walk around the outside.

"I'm not sure how to broach this," Dr. Gold says carefully as our steps crunch on the gravel path.

"You can be blunt," I tell her flatly. "It would be a change from everyone in there."

"Well, I appreciate that," she says. "Now, Cora . . . I can't imagine how hard this is for you. After his family, you were the closest to him."

I clench my jaw. "We were friends really fast."

"Yes." She hesitates and then goes on. "I don't know if Adrien ever told you about his time at Pomegranate."

"He said he was interviewed by the Golden Department," I say honestly.

"Yes," she says, sounding relieved. As if she had been worried it was some secret. "He was an interesting subject, to say the least. Perhaps even a little unwilling."

I smile. "Sounds right."

"Well . . ." She brushes her fingers along the stone statues that we pass. "Cora, this is really hard to say. Hard to explain. But we have Adrien. At Pomegranate."

I stop walking. I stare at my feet and wait for her to go on. I can't walk and listen to this at the same time, and I really have to hear her. I stare at the cheap black pumps Dad got me for Mum's funeral. I wonder if I'll have to wear them to another one soon.

"What do you mean you have him at Pomegranate?"

She smiles at me. A hopeful smile. "Cora, we made a Gram of him. A pretty good one too. We have him. At Pomegranate. Ready."

It's so utterly life-changing. He's there. Not gone after all, his mind alive in a computer, still here and waiting.

In the Waiting Rooms. At Pomegranate.

I feel my jaw start to tremble, so violently that I'm worried it might detach completely. I'm too overwhelmed to be ashamed. It's so painfully hopeful.

"I can see him again? As he was?"

I stagger to sit down on a wooden bench. A golden plaque on it with a dedication to someone who passed away years ago. My eyes are so blurry, I can't read the name. Dr. Gold sits down beside me.

"It would be a lot, emotionally," she says delicately. "But yes. You could see him again."

I gasp for air. The full impact of what Pomegranate really is hits me like a train.

"But . . ." I feel abashed to say it, but it has to be said. "I can't afford Pomegranate prices. The expense . . . to run the Grams. I couldn't afford it."

"Well, I was thinking about that," Dr. Gold says caringly. "I'll discuss it with Magnus. Not today, obviously. But later. If you let the Golden Department interview you for research purposes . . . we could let you visit with Adrien's Gram as payment."

Hope thunders through me like electric shocks. "Then I'll do it."

"Well, your dad—"

"I'm doing it."

She sighs but smiles at me. "I love your spirit, Cora." I feel all the hurt, all the difficulty of the day, rush through me and I'm hugging her. Clinging on to her like I'm caught in a storm and she's the only solid object among the cold, crashing waves.

"It's okay, Cora," she whispers, squeezing me tightly. "It's all okay."

"I don't think I'll ever be happy again," I breathe.

"I know you feel that now," she says firmly. "But you will. It's all-consuming now. That's how I felt after my mum. But it softens. It fades."

She rolls her sleeve up and shows me a faint white scar. Like an icicle on her wrist.

"This cut wouldn't stop bleeding when I cut it as a kid. I was climbing a fence and slipped. It was so messy and painful, I never thought it would stop. But it did. And it got better. And now it's just some faint scar."

I stare at her skin. Adrien will never be a faint scar. Neither will Mum. But I understand what she's trying to say.

I look back to the hospital. I can see the reception area. The automatic doors opening and closing. I can see Ria Hawkins just outside it smoking and speaking to Magnus.

He isn't looking at her and the more animated she is, the more rigid he becomes. He eventually walks away from her.

"Would Mr. and Mrs. Hawkins really be all right with me seeing Adrien again? Like that?" I ask Dr. Gold, not taking my eyes from a now-hysterical Ria. She's inaudible behind the faraway glass, but I can still hear her cries somehow.

"If you agreed to help Pomegranate"—Dr. Gold squeezes my shoulder, looking over at the same sight—"they would be more than happy. I promise."

HOW DID YOU SPEND YOUR SUMMER?

We're sitting around the dinner table, at home. I'm still thinking about my conversation with Dr. Gold while Dad and Gregor fuss over the food. I can tell that they're both completely panicked about me. Worried I'll have a complete breakdown. Dad's made a huge chicken with garlic and herbs, and Gregor has cooked every single one of my favorite side dishes. We're drinking pink lemonade and Dad has put gentle classical music on.

"This all looks delicious," I say honestly.

Dad breathes an enormous sigh of relief and he and Gregor exchange looks of satisfaction. I wait until they have both taken big bites of chicken before I speak.

"I'm going to be interviewed at Pomegranate."

Dad starts to cough, suddenly choking a little on his dinner. Gregor gulps down some lemonade and glances fearfully at me.

"What?" Dad says hoarsely, rapidly pouring some water for himself and clearing his throat.

"It's not up for discussion," I say firmly. "I'm doing it."

"Cora." Gregor, who was always in favor of this, looks hesitant and a little ashen. "I'm not sure that's the best thing for you right now."

"It is one hundred percent not the best thing for you right now," Dad snaps sharply. "It's the last thing you should be doing, given the circumstances. You've been through a massive shock."

"Dad, I'm not discussing it," I say gently. "It's decided. I've agreed to do it."

"That man cornered you at his own son's hospital bed?" Dad says quietly, in a deadly tone. "I've never thought much of him, but that's too low."

"He did not," I shoot back, glaring at Dad. "He barely had a moment to himself the whole time, and Mrs. Hawkins was losing it. He didn't ask me. I want to do it."

"Cora, you should use the summer to rest and relax," Gregor says softly. Running a hand through his tousled hair. "You don't want to be cooped up in that place. It's the very start of your summer holidays, you should be having fun."

"I'm really tired of everyone telling me what I want and how I should feel," I say stiffly. "You did this when Mum died. I'm doing it. I've scheduled the first session with Dr. Gold on Monday. I'd like a lift to Canary Wharf for eleven but if you don't want to, I'll get the bus. But no matter what either of you think, I'm doing it."

I cut up my chicken and pour some gravy over it before taking a generous bite. I chew daintily while the two of them stare at me. They've been treading so carefully around me since it happened, and I've obviously unsettled them with my announcement.

I'm sure they'd be even more unsettled if they knew why I have decided to do it.

I just eat my food and consider the matter closed.

*

Gregor parks the car outside Pomegranate but catches me by the wrist as I reach to let myself out.

"I know what they've promised you, Cora." I freeze. And wait.

"They've got a Gram of Adrien."

It's not a question but a statement. Of course Gregor would know, he works for them.

"Yes," I say anyway.

"They'll let you visit with the Gram if you let them study you?"

"Yes."

"Cora." He fidgets in his seat, glancing at the large front entrance of the Pomegranate building. "I don't know about this."

"You work for them, Gregor." I laugh as I say it because he's being so serious. "If you don't agree with it, why do you work for them?"

"I just do some programming," he replies, his forehead wrinkled in concern. "But this won't be like meeting a celebrity Gram, Cora. It won't be like that at all."

"I know," I snap. "Okay? I still want to do it."

I open the car door and walk up the steps to the front doors, not turning around to check if he's following me. Noma, the receptionist, looks up as soon as she hears me.

"I've got a company pass for you," she says shrilly, gesturing to a lanyard that lies flat on the white marble desk. It has a golden outline. "Don't lose it."

"I won't."

"Dr. Gold is waiting in her office."

I nod. I glance back to see Gregor still sitting in the car, staring at the steering wheel. I feel a rush of empathy for him, but I don't know what to say. I don't know what he and Dad want to hear.

I get into the elevator and place the lanyard around my neck.

The elevator soars up, seamless and swift. Not like the elevators at the hospital, which are clunky and awkward. I'm nervous and anxious but remind myself that once this session is over, I'll get to see my best friend again.

It's been two weeks since that day. But it feels like two years.

I just want to see my friend again. As he was.

The doors slide open and I enter an unfamiliar floor. It's completely silent, not filled with a buzz of conversation like on the marketing floor or the tech floor. I find an intimidating black door with Dr. Gold's name printed on it.

I knock.

"Come in?"

I push the door open and nervously step inside. She's behind her desk, glasses on and hair tied up. She seems engrossed in something she's reading on her tablet but upon seeing that it's me, she puts it firmly to one side.

"Cora."

I take in the room. A shelf of ornaments and trinkets. Awards that people have given Dr. Gold. She gets up from her desk and makes her way toward me. I drag my eyes from the shining objects to look at her.

She hugs me and I flinch at first and then allow it. She steps back, still holding me by the shoulders.

"I'm so glad you're doing this," she says, eyes shining. "It's going to help so many people."

"I'm nervous," I admit as she steers me out of her office and down the long, silent corridor.

"Of course you are." I'm glad she doesn't tell me not to be or that I'm being silly. "That's perfectly all right." We reach an interview room. Just like Adrien told me.

White, so very white. With a large mirror on the wall.

Dr. Gold sits in one seat and I automatically sit opposite her.

"Do you want some water?" she asks me genially.

"No, thank you."

"Okay. We're just going to wait for Dr. Connelly to come and then we can start. It will be recorded, if that's all right?"

I swallow and glance around once again at the pristine whiteness of the room. "That's fine."

She gives an almost-imperceptible nod to the mirror on the wall.

I know there are people watching me behind that mirror. People I can't see but know are there. Because Adrien warned me.

"How are you feeling?"

I look away from my somewhat pale face in the mirror and back to Dr. Gold. She has her tablet and a stylus on her lap and is smiling at me expectantly.

I never know how to answer questions like that. Nonautistic people will ask you how you are constantly, but they usually mean it as a greeting. If I ever actually answer the question honestly, they get uncomfortable quickly.

"I'm fine," I murmur.

She arches her perfectly plucked eyebrows and smiles gently. "Cora, you don't have to mask in these interviews. It's important to just be yourself."

I don't think nonautistic people really understand what they're asking when they want you to unmask. But perhaps that's why I'm here. To let them understand.

The door suddenly flies open and a stout man in very informal clothing bustles in. He's carrying a tablet with a coffee cup balanced on it like it's a tray. He nods briefly at me and then takes his seat next to Dr. Gold. Her face is difficult to read but she moves her chair ever so slightly so that she's not sitting so close to him.

"Sorry I'm late," he says crisply. "I'm Dr. Connelly. Have you started?"

"We're just chatting," Dr. Gold says silkily, waiting until he's transfixed with his coffee once more before rolling her eyes and grinning at me.

I grin back.

"Right." Dr. Connelly finally settles and looks over at me with a somewhat piercing look. "Nora. Just some questions to start."

"Sure," I say swiftly. "But my name is Cora."

He blinks at me and Dr. Gold laughs, her whole body alive with humor as she scoots her chair a little closer to me.

"Do you know what makes you different, Cora? Could you tell us?"

And I take a deep breath. Trying to remember. Why I'm doing this.

For Adrien. To see Adrien again.

THE WAITING ROOM

"I don't think of myself as different."

I say it confidently but keeping eye contact is hard. Dr. Gold looks a little disappointed, but she leans forward, smiling empathetically. "But you're autistic?"

"Yes. But lots of people are."

"Of course," she says quickly. "Yes."

"It's natural." I shrug, scratching a patch of eczema on my wrist.

"It is," Dr. Gold agrees carefully, and I can tell that she's thinking hard about what to say. Dr. Connelly glances at the mirror and then back to Dr. Gold.

"Have you ever met another autistic person?"

"Well, no," I say truthfully. "But some people don't know they are. And my best friend has ADHD. They're under the same umbrella."

Her face softens. "Do you mean Adrien?"

"Yes. He has ADHD."

Dr. Connelly writes something down on his tablet. I wish I were closer so I could read it.

"How would you describe having autism?" Dr. Connelly asks his first question, not looking at me.

"Well, I wouldn't describe it like that."

Grief is so strange. Second time around, I'm far less polite. The filter just isn't as strong anymore. I don't care what people think of me.

Well, I care about Dr. Gold. But she actually sees me.

More than most people.

"What do you mean?"

"I mean, I'm autistic."

"Oh." Dr. Connelly makes a strange sympathetic noise. "No, you have autism. You should put yourself first. Person with autism."

"Um."

"We say person with cancer, not cancerous person. Do you see? You should put yourself before your condition."

"I don't have cancer."

"Let's try another question," Dr. Gold says sharply, cutting Dr. Connelly a look of disdain. "What does it feel like to be you, Cora?"

That's a much better question. And one people never ask me.

"Right now?" I ask.

I think of planes in the sky. Of Cerby's wet nose. Hot pasta dinners. The roses in Hyde Park. Lloyd blasting the radio and rolling down the windows. Fierce laughter that is sometimes so overpowering, you don't even make a sound. You're just doubled over, eyes shut tight and gasping for air.

I think of dancing in a conga line around the school hall.

"Please be honest," Dr. Gold adds gingerly.

Two pinkies locked together. Together against the ordinary world.

"Right now, I feel empty."

*

Adrien used to say that when he was burning out, he would go on autopilot. Basic functions. If he was worn out by other people, he would go through the motions just to get by. That's what I do for the remainder of the interview. I give basic answers. Luckily, they seem to satisfy Dr. Connelly.

I'm not so sure about Dr. Gold. But as she leads me to the fourth floor, the Waiting Rooms, she seems pleased with me.

"Thank you again for doing this," she says gently as we reach an electric-blue door. "It's set up in here. Once you're ready to begin, just say 'show' and the technicians will start."

"Okay."

"And, Cora?"

I look up at her, but she bends down so that we are level.

"This might be really hard at first. Really overwhelming. And it's important that you don't break the illusion for the Gram."

"No, I know," I assure her. "I won't, I promise."

She smiles and presses her hand against my face. "I know you won't."

She knocks once on the blue door and then turns the handle, pushing it ajar for me. I step forward, both eager and terrified.

It's nothing like seeing a celebrity Gram. It's nothing like anything I've ever experienced.

My brain knows that I'm looking at a hologram, carefully re-created to represent a human being. The logical part of me knows it to be true.

But every other part of me feels like I'm seeing a ghost.

He is frozen, waiting for the technicians to start the simulation. I sit across from him, unable to look away.

Every single detail is replicated perfectly. The nose, the eyebrows. The eyes are closed, waiting for my signal. I take a moment. I feel strangely nervous. Parts of me are still rebelling against what I am witnessing, crying out at the impossibility.

But the hope is the strongest. "Show."

It's a strangled, unsure sound but wherever they are, the technicians hear it. Adrien's eyes open.

We stare at each other. And everything I wanted to say has gone away.

His face breaks into a smile and I can feel my eyes getting wet.

"You don't seem happy to see me?"

I let out a whoosh of air and my head bows, my nails digging into my knees. I feel like I've just run up a hill and forgotten to breathe. So, upon reaching the top, I'm desperately trying to catch my breath.

"I'm very happy to see you," I croak roughly, not looking up yet.

"Yeah, you look really happy," the hologram that is Adrien says, laughing.

"No, I am," I say quickly, looking up at the bright lights attached to rigging in the ceiling. All working together to project this re-creation, this digital soul. "I'm very happy."

"Well, good. Nothing worse than a misery moan."

I bark out a laugh and finally look at him. The Gram is a masterpiece. More real than I ever could have dreamed.

"So." He splays his lifelike hands out in front of him. "Who are you?"

MRS. HAWKINS WON'T BE JOINING US

"I should have prepared you, Cora, I'm so sorry."

"It's fine," I tell Dr. Gold, my head between my legs as I listen to the cool and gentle water in the Peace Garden on the ground floor of Pomegranate. "I should have put two and two together."

"His Gram was finalized about a year ago now," she explains. "He was one of our earliest sign-offs."

"Before we met."

"Exactly. I'm so sorry, I should have remembered."

"It's fine."

The meeting had been cut short. They must have noticed my shock at not being recognized. Shock because it had felt so normal, so familiar, and everything had come flooding back.

"I'll be more prepared for next time," I say sternly. I'm not going to let them take these sessions away.

"I'm amazed you convinced your dad to sign the consent forms," Dr. Gold says, changing the subject. "From everything your brother tells me, he's dead set against this place."

"He is," I acknowledge. "And I'm not completely sure why."

Also, Gregor was the one who signed them. But I don't tell her this.

"When we fully open to the public, we'll have an Empathy Department."

"Oh, yeah?"

"People trained to help settle and prepare people properly for how overwhelming Pomegranate, and my department, can be. And will be."

I watch one happy fish swim in the clear pond, going in a different direction from all the others. "But people will have to pay money to see the Grams?"

"Well, of course," Dr. Gold says, shrugging gently. "This place is expensive. We need a lot of staff. Nothing good is ever really free these days."

I keep watching the fish. Watch it alone on the far end of the pond, poking its nose against the wet stones. As if it's trying to get out.

*

"Gregor, this is going to be the most awkward thing."

"I know," my brother shoots back at me, barely moving

his mouth as he speaks. "But Magnus invited us. Insisted, actually. I could hardly say no. And if you want them to put you on the visitor list for Adrien, you need to make an appearance. Besides, Dad's working tonight so I can't leave you home alone."

Gregor rings the doorbell to Adrien's house. I can hear Cerby barking.

Magnus answers, which surprises us both. "Where's Bella?" I ask, and Gregor pinches me.

"She quit," Magnus says plainly, showing us into the sitting room and shaking Gregor's hand so vigorously, it looks painful.

I glance around the house as I sit in the familiar room. It's the same. Not changed in any remarkable way. But there's definitely a different feel to the place.

"How was your first session with Dr. Gold, Cora?" Magnus asks, pouring Gregor a drink, which he should refuse, as he's driving. "She said it went well?"

Gregor doesn't refuse the drink. But he doesn't sip from it either.

"It was fine," I say truthfully. "I think it was just some introductory stuff to begin with, Mr. Hawkins."

"Excellent. Good."

A strange silence. I glance around the large room, wondering when Ria will appear. It seems so quiet. No sound of her heels, no trace of her perfume.

Magnus catches me looking and pours himself a second

drink. "Mrs. Hawkins won't be joining us, Cora. She's not feeling well."

"Understandably," Gregor says, and then he winces, like he forgot to filter for a moment.

I'm in the firm headspace I need to make small talk, so I won't make mistakes like that. I pat his arm, though. I suddenly hear thumps on the stairs and then the clatter of nails as Cerby comes bounding into the room. He barks in triumph upon seeing me and leaps on me in a friendly attack. I laugh between licks and firmly clap my hands against his belly to keep him happy.

Gregor reaches out to pet him, but he's already trying to climb onto the sofa next to me.

"Do you want him, Cora?" Magnus asks suddenly.

I look up. "Sorry?"

"The dog? You can take him home with you, if you like."

I'm having a hard time understanding what I can hear in his tone. I look down at Cerby's lovely, friendly face and then back to Adrien's father, who is staring into his glass.

"Don't you want him, Mr. Hawkins?" I ask quietly.

He scoffs. "That dog was always a fight between the boy and me."

Cerby settles next to me and nuzzles his wet nose against the crook of my elbow.

"Good friend of mine is a breeder," Magnus adds, putting some ice into his glass. "Beautiful dogs. They place every year in the gun dog category at shows. He had a wonderful old girl give birth to a litter and we wanted one of the pups for Adrien."

He sips from his glass and fixes Cerby with a frightening look. It almost makes me want to pull the dog closer, but then it's gone. His face is neutral again. "But Adrien wanted that thing. Found him in Battersea. Couldn't be talked out of it."

He slams the glass down on the coffee table and crosses one leg over the other.

"I said, 'The thing has fleas, son. Get a pedigree. Get something pure, something built properly.' But no, he wanted the mongrel."

I look down at said mongrel. Knowing his wonderful nature, his unquestionable loyalty. Remembering how much Adrien adored him.

And I pull him closer.

We suddenly hear a little movement upstairs. I glance up at the ceiling.

"She won't eat," Magnus suddenly says matter-of-factly.

"I'll take something up for her, Mr. Hawkins."

I volunteer because the feeling in the room is so cold and unpleasant. I don't know what to say, what to expect. I hate when grown-ups are unpredictable, it's when they're at their most scary.

I get up and move into the kitchen. I can hear Gregor

and Mr. Hawkins discussing Pomegranate business as I open the enormous fridge.

I find a plate and put together some cold cuts of meat, some salmon, cut up some sourdough bread. A few olives and a snap of dark chocolate. I take the plate up the stairs and pause on the landing, outside the main bedroom.

I know it's the main bedroom, though I've never been in it. You don't go into your best friend's parents' bedroom. It's an unspoken rule of any house you visit.

I knock.

There's a long gap before I hear "Come in."

I push the door open, careful to balance the plate and not drop the food all over the pristine white carpet.

The bedroom feels bigger than our entire downstairs. There's two walk-in wardrobes and I find Ria in hers. It's more white carpet, with lots of mirrors and fairy lights all over the walls and ceiling.

She's lying on her side on the floor. No shoes on. "I've brought you something to eat, Mrs. Hawkins," I say, sitting down next to her and tucking my feet under me. I lay the plate down gently next to her. She looks so much younger without her makeup on.

She looks at the plate and her eyebrows arch in surprise. "That actually looks good."

I smile. I push the plate toward her and feel relief as she nibbles on the salmon.

"Sorry that I'm not very sociable this evening," she says, and her voice sounds very husky and dry.

"That's all right," I tell her. "I don't like being sociable either, really."

She takes a little of the bread. "Yes, I remember forcing you out to find Adrien the first time you came over."

I laugh. "Well, it was better than being stuck with the grown-ups."

"I don't care for any of them much either."

After she says it, she regards me carefully. I let her, looking down at the olives on the plate.

"What happened to your mum?"

No one ever asks. I went back to school, after she died, and it was obvious that the teacher had told everyone beforehand not to say a thing about it. I came back after some time away and they all acted like I had been on holiday.

"She was sick, and she just didn't get better."

Ria nods slowly. "Do you still feel her around?"

I think for a moment. I don't know how to answer that. For the days after she died, it often felt like she was in the next room. It didn't seem real. But now, as time has passed, it feels more final.

"Sometimes," I settle on. "When I'm with people who knew her too."

"I bet she'd be really proud of you," Ria says steadily. "You're smart. And Adrien loved you so much."

I definitely don't know what to say to that.

"I just want to talk about him all the time," she goes on, smiling wanly. "All the time. I want to tell every person I see on the street about him. But no one will speak about him with me, because they don't know what to say."

I look at the huge diamond ring on her long, slender finger. "I know."

"The morning of that day"—she gets to a sitting position and tosses her hair over her shoulder—"he told me all about what you got up to at the British Museum."

I must be a certain shade of red because she laughs and taps one of my cheeks with her finger.

"He was a bad influence," I joke. "In a good way."

"Yes," she laughs.

We sit for a moment, completely still.

"I know every parent says this," she finally whispers, releasing the words like they're wishes, "but he was special. He was better. He could make his mind work in ways other people couldn't. He was never made for rows in a classroom or standard tests or homework. He always had to ask why. Always needed to know how everything worked. The clock on the wall, the hinges on the door. He was . . . brilliant."

I am holding my breath. "Is. He *is* brilliant."

Her face crumples for a nanosecond, like a glass breaking. Then she composes herself. "Yes. Is. You're right."

"He's just asleep."

She doesn't react. I twist my body, uncomfortable with the silence. Not knowing how to make it better.

"I read once," I hear myself saying, "that people in comas are going on adventures in their minds. In some other land. And once they've completed their adventure, done what they need to do, they might come back."

She drags a finger along the white carpet, head bowed with strands of hair covering her face.

"He could do anything he put his mind to," I remind her. "So, whatever it is he needs to do, wherever he is . . . he'll manage it. And he'll come back."

She smiles. Barely there. But definitely there. "Thank you for bringing this up," she eventually says softly.

I wonder if she means the subject of conversation and then realize she's talking about the food. "It's okay, Mrs. Hawkins."

"Come on." She nods at the door. "I'll walk you back down to the grown-ups."

She holds my hand as we go down the staircase and I don't mind it. She squeezes it as we reach the hallway. Gregor and Magnus are at the door to the dining room and both look surprised to see us.

"You got her out of her room," Mr. Hawkins says jovially. "Well done, Cora."

"Enjoy your evening," Ria tells Gregor coolly.

She squeezes my hand one more time and begins heading back upstairs.

"If you ever need someone to babysit Cora," Magnus tells Gregor, "please feel free to drop her off here. She's very welcome. Ria doesn't have a job, and she'll need the company with Bella gone and only that stupid dog." Ria stops halfway up the stairs and turns her head slightly so that we hear her speak, even though it's quiet.

"I had a job. For thirteen years."

I watch her back as she ascends, not giving any of us a look at her face.

"I still do," she calls down before shutting her bedroom door, sharply.

Cerby whines from his basket by the kitchen.

I feel cold. Cold except for my hand, still warm from her touch.

BEHIND THE MIRROR

"My name's Cora."

It's the strangest thing, introducing myself to him again. It's different this time around. We're not in the garden and I haven't just knocked him to the ground.

"Adrien."

"Nice to meet you."

He makes a face, which makes me laugh. "You're very serious, Cora."

"Am not."

"Are."

I giggle. It feels slightly euphoric, to be sitting here with him again. Gregor made sure to say on the way here that it wasn't really him, once again. But he doesn't get it. It is him. It's his mind. Uploaded. Remade.

It really is him.

"I saw your mum last night," I tell him.

His face changes. He suddenly looks worried. "Is she okay?"

For a moment, I feel like he knows. Like he understands. But I shake that away. "She's fine." Maybe not completely true, but I have to keep up the illusion. "I made her a plate of food and she ate most of it."

"So how do you know my mum?"

It hurts. I can't say that it doesn't. I want to tell him everything. That we're best friends. That we met on his birthday. That I knew Bella and Cerby. And Lloyd. And that he's told me all about his uncle Max.

"We met at a party."

"That makes sense," he says laughingly. "Mum's always throwing parties. And going to them. I used to hide her perfume and hairbrush when I was little to keep her at home."

I stare in wonder. Memories. He may not know me, but he seems to remember things. Everything. It's extraordinary.

"Was the party good?"

His question jars me back into the room. "It was all right. A lot of older people and I don't really like meeting new faces all at once."

"Me neither," he says. I notice that he is much more still now. I'm used to him constantly moving, even when he's giving you all his attention. There's usually a knee jiggling. Not now, he's perfectly at ease. "I can tell as soon as I meet someone whether I'll like them or not."

That sounds exactly like him. And the way his voice is replicated is so natural, I have to remind myself that it is a re-creation. That there is no breath. No air in the lungs. Just clever code and projection, and a chip. That's what I managed to get Gregor to reveal. Each Gram has their own chip with all their data stored on it. While the data is backed up on the system, the chip is essential for the permanent interactivity of the Gram.

We talk. About things that don't seem important. I tell him about the time I almost burned the house down making toast. It makes him laugh. Like it did the first time I told him. He tells me about some school days. Except he tells it differently. But I don't mind.

Dr. Gold knocks on the door to let me know that my session time is coming to an end. I take a heavy breath and smile at the Gram, wishing I could explain everything.

"See you soon."

He smiles back. "See you soon." And then he freezes. And disappears.

I wonder what's happening in the control room. What it's like to bring someone back to life for a moment.

"Was it better this time?" Dr. Gold asks as she walks me downstairs.

"Yes," I say brightly. "Much."

When we reach the lobby, her phone starts to ring. She cancels the call and frowns at her screen.

"These hideous investors," she says offhandedly. "They want every waking minute of my life right now. Vultures."

She chucks me once under the chin and smiles. "See you at our next interview."

"Okay," I say, watching her go. I wait until she's out of sight and then turn straight back around.

I go to the elevator, clasping my access lanyard protectively.

Luckily, Noma is on a call with her back to me.

"I'm sorry," she says carefully, to whoever is on the other end of the call. "But at present, Pomegranate does not create Grams of pets. Pets are not currently offered as packages from our Golden Department. Well, I'm sorry. No, it's just not possible. I'm very sorry, please don't cry."

I step inside the elevator and press the floor I need. Feeling terrified and excited. I don't know if it's the motion of the elevator making my stomach jump, or if it's exhilaration.

*

I reach the floor where the Waiting Rooms are located, the one we've just left. I face the quiet, empty corridor.

I know the different-colored doors all lead to Waiting

Rooms, but I start to check anyway. Each one is like a soothing, comfortable hotel room. Slightly different in style but all sticking to a similar pattern.

So where do the technicians go?

I'm at a loss when I hear voices. I wrench open the closest Waiting Room door and throw myself inside, pulling the door behind me. Keeping it ajar, I peer through the tiny gap and my mouth falls open.

Two technicians, wearing the same jacket Gregor is required to wear, exit the Waiting Room I was just in with Adrien. But how can they be leaving that room when they weren't in there with us and there's no other door?

I pull back as they walk by, careful not to be seen. "Poor kid," one says to the other as they make their way down the corridor toward the elevator.

"Don't be soft," laughs the other, pressing the button that calls the elevator. "Won't last long around here if you start feeling sorry for them."

I blanch at that, holding my breath until I hear them go inside.

Once the doors close, I dash down the corridor to the room they've just left. When I step inside, everything is exactly how I left it.

So then where did they come from?

I lock onto the mirror. It takes up almost the entire wall. But not the whole wall. I squeeze myself against the wall and tuck my hand behind the mirror and pull. Every inch of me tenses, terrified that the whole thing will detach from the plaster, fall to the ground and shatter, the sound alerting the Pomegranate staff.

But that doesn't happen. It opens like a door.

To reveal an intricate and dazzling control room. I let out a puff of air as I step inside, pulling the strange mirror door behind me. It clicks neatly into place. Sure enough, I can see into the Waiting Room from the other side of the mirror. This little control room is hidden.

It feels strange now, knowing the sessions are being watched with such closeness. I look at the computer equipment. While I don't understand any of it, and am afraid to touch, I know that this is what must keep Gregor working here. It's the kind of nerdy stuff he's always dreamed about. I'm kind of happy for him, looking at all the switches and dials.

There are two leather seats on swivels, facing the mirror. The technicians must sit here while the Waiting Room sessions are going on.

I'm about to start looking for where they keep the Gram's chips when I freeze.

The door to the Waiting Room opens and someone comes in. I watch through the mirror, petrified until I remember that I can see them, not the other way around.

It's Magnus Hawkins.

He shuts the Waiting Room door with his foot and sits down on the seat I was using while talking to Adrien. He puts a Tupperware box of cold pasta and a mug of coffee on the table.

Then he gets up and starts moving toward the mirror. I gasp and leap back, just able to conceal myself behind one of the large leather chairs, desperately hoping he doesn't see my legs in the dark.

If he catches me, it's over.

I can hear him fumbling around with the control board, and then a click. I wish I could see but I can't risk giving away my position. Only when I hear the mirror close do I look up.

Adrien's Gram has reappeared. It's not awake. He's frozen in his usual place. Magnus doesn't seem to mind, though. He sits back in the seat opposite Adrien and starts eating his food. I get to my feet, never taking my eyes away from the strange scene.

Mr. Hawkins doesn't say a word to the frozen Gram.

He just eats. Quietly.

I watch, knowing that he may come back into the room on this side of the mirror at any moment. Until the Waiting Room door opens for a second time.

Dr. Gold enters. She doesn't look surprised to see Mr. Hawkins here.

"Thank you for knocking," Mr. Hawkins says dryly. He doesn't turn around to look at her, just keeps eating.

Dr. Gold watches the back of his head. I watch her. I always look at her when we're together, she's one of the only adults I feel comfortable with around here. One of the only ones I can look in the eye.

"You don't want me to animate him for you?"

"No." Mr. Hawkins sips his coffee and glances fleetingly at the motionless Gram. "Thank you."

"Her session went well, apparently." She's talking about me. "She's good about keeping the illusion going." Her praise fills me up like the biggest meal. "I thought you'd want to know. I know you were concerned that kids might be problematic when we open."

"Normal kids still might be."

"I'm not so sure. We can still set an age limit, but I think kids her age will be fine."

"You two seem very chummy."

Mr. Hawkins still won't look at her while he speaks. He chooses each piece of pasta carefully before skewering it with his fork.

"We are."

"Strange. Thought you didn't like kids."

"Well, she's like a little adult."

She suddenly glances at the mirror and I clap my hand over my mouth to stop a gasp. It feels like she's looking right at me, but I know she cannot see me.

"When's your next interview?"

"Tomorrow."

"Good. I have some questions for you to ask."

At that, he throws his things into the small wastebasket

close to the sitting area. He then leaves the room, moving quickly by Dr. Gold, all without a glance. She watches him go and looks agitated. I hold my breath, wondering if she'll come into the control room to close down Adrien's Gram.

She doesn't. She leaves too.

I wait, breathing heavily, until I know they're both well and truly gone. Then I move toward the control panel in search of Adrien's chip.

I find it plugged into the main system. It appears to be the size of a credit card.

With his name written on it.

I stare at it. A whole soul, a whole mind, a lifetime of memories.

On that one little thing.

AMISS

The next few sessions with Dr. Gold and Dr. Connelly are rigorous. They have me on a treadmill, reading Dickens aloud, eating when I'm wide awake and again when I'm really tired. Dr. Connelly will ask me to recite something from memory and then fire random questions at me while I try to do so. I have to walk on a line on the floor, demonstrate balance as well as throwing and catching.

Then the questions. The endless gunfire of questions. It's like being diagnosed all over again, except they're way more insistent. More detailed. They ask me every possible question under the sun.

After five days of it, I start to dread the sessions.

"So how does it work?" I ask as Friday arrives and we're starting another day of sessions. "Do you compare all my answers to a nonautistic person's and then focus on the differences?"

Dr. Gold smiles at me. "Precisely."

"Okay." I take a bite of an apple that has been brought for me, knowing that the way I am eating it is being recorded. "But I'm only one autistic person. We're all different. We're not all the same."

"No, we know," Dr. Gold says supportively. "But it's an excellent start for our research. We still have to perfect everything before we can open to the public."

"And you'll charge people to come?"

"Well, yes. And a small fee if someone volunteers to undergo the process. The interview process, I mean. To become a Gram."

"What Adrien did?"

"Yes, exactly."

"I suppose it is a lot of work."

"Well, you're getting a taste of it," Dr. Gold says, laughing and poking me gently with her stylus.

"We want to talk more about memory today," Dr. Connelly says, interrupting our conversation.

I exhale. Knowing I just have to get to lunchtime and then I can see Adrien. "Fine."

"What's your earliest memory?"

I bristle at the question. Memory is funny for me. Some things are vivid and clear, others are as if it happened to somebody else.

"My dad was at a bowling alley for a work party. He couldn't leave me and my brother home alone, so we were there as well. The bowling alley was in a rec center. And I looked down from a window in the alley to a swimming pool on the floor below. And someone was swimming laps."

Dr. Connelly looks at me with surprise and then glances at Dr. Gold, who doesn't say anything. "That's a very . . . specific first memory, Cora."

"Do you want something more interesting?" I snap. "Okay, Dr. Connelly. I opened my eyes and saw three faces smiling down at me, Mum, Dad and Gregor. And they were all so happy to see me and the sun was shining down behind them and everyone was really, really happy. And birds were singing, and music was playing, and we were all together. All of us. And really happy."

I don't know why I feel like crying. Why do I always do this? Why, when I feel backed into a corner, do I always come out swinging? They're scratching at the surface of me, demanding to know what's underneath. Do they know how horrible it then feels to see them frown and shake their heads?

Show us who you are. No, not like that.

I've always had to laugh when people say "Be yourself." They have no idea. Not in the slightest.

I like myself. I like the way my brain works. But there is just something about walking into a room full of people, who aren't like you and will never know what it feels like to be you, that breaks you down. It would take too long to explain it to them. That's if they even cared to know in the first place.

I miss Mum. I feel like I'm not allowed to say that now. As if grief has some sort of use-by date that you can't go beyond. For a while, I tried to ration the time I spent thinking about her. Whenever it rained, I would allow myself to remember. I would watch the water come down and use that time to feel everything. But you can't spend your life waiting for the rain. Resenting the sun.

I miss her. All the time. It's just how it is.

And I miss Adrien. Even though he's technically still here.

His brain worked differently. We weren't exactly the same, but somehow, he just knew. He knew what it felt like. We never had to explain ourselves.

He showed up in my life like the answer to a question.

Is there anyone out there like me? Anyone?

"I think she's tired," Dr. Gold says softly to Dr. Connelly, putting her tablet away. "Cora, we've definitely been demanding of you this week. Why don't you take a break and when you're ready, you can see Adrien?"

I bite my lip to stop a slight tremble and nod enthusiastically, grateful to Dr. Gold in ways she can never know. I get up and throw my apple in the wastebasket on my way out of the interview room.

*

"Do you ever get scared of turning into a grown-up?"

I ask Adrien the question as we sit in our Pomegranate Waiting Room. He ponders the question and shrugs.

"Sometimes. Especially when I look at my parents."

"You know, everyone turns into their parents. Gregor gets more like our dad every day."

"I definitely don't want to turn into my dad."

I'm about to say that without Magnus, Pomegranate might not exist, but I stop myself just in time.

"Your dad is a bit like my mum," I say instead. "Their work is everything to them and it tires them out. Makes them less capable of being cheerful at home."

"You're lucky you're not an only child," he replies. "I'm either being ganged up on or I'm stuck in the middle."

I don't know if it's because I'm so tired, but there's something strange about Adrien's Gram. The more he has begun to learn about me, the more I've become a part of his increasing memory and mind, the more distant he seems. I wonder if Grams can get tired just like we do.

"What about your uncle Max?"

"What about him? Only met him once, years ago at Mum's birthday."

I stare. Confused. "What?"

"At Mum's birthday. Years ago. He stopped by for a bit

and then left. Got in an argument with Dad about something. He's nothing special."

I continue to gape at him. "Nothing special? But you love him."

He gives me a quizzical look. "Hold on, Cora. You don't have to love someone just because they're family." Something isn't right. In fact, something is very wrong.

Adrien adored his uncle. The feeling was very mutual. They had a secret handshake. They went flying together. They talked on the phone every day when Adrien had chicken pox. Adrien was always talking about Max.

"Flying is a special interest of yours, isn't it?" I prompt, remembering the conversation we had in his garden. "Isn't it?"

He nods and I feel a twinge of relief. Glad that we're back on track.

"Yeah."

"Good," I laugh, comforted.

"I'd love to have lessons someday."

The comfort vanishes. Adrien was having his flying lessons long before he was interviewed by Pomegranate. Long before he met me.

"I mean," he goes on, "I know it's impossible, hardly anyone flies nowadays, but I still would love to learn. People do give lessons, in those little tiny planes. I'd love to try it."

"But you have tried it!" I cry out, before I can stop myself.

"What?"

"Adrien, you've been flying. You've been lots of times." He looks at me, trying to process what I'm saying, and then suddenly freezes. I make a noise of frustration and turn to glare at the mirror.

The technicians in the booth must have called for reinforcement, because Magnus Hawkins suddenly enters the room. "What happened?" he asks stiffly.

"Why doesn't he remember his flying lessons?" I demand. "Or his uncle Max?"

Something flickers on Mr. Hawkins's face, but he shakes it away and gives me a stern look. "He will remember. It's probably just a minor glitch. Thank you for drawing our attention to it, Cora, but you can't take out your frustrations about little things like that on the Gram."

"I wasn't."

"You've been really mature about your sessions, I would hate for you to lose them."

I hear the veiled threat and bite my tongue. He nods at the mirror and the Gram starts up again.

The moment Adrien catches sight of Magnus, his face changes. It opens up and his eyes widen.

"Hi, Dad."

Magnus has almost reached the door of the Waiting

Room, intending to leave. He hesitates and glances back over his shoulder. "Just heading to work, son."

"Can't you talk for a bit? You can meet Cora, she's my friend."

I can see Magnus's hand tighten on the door handle. He won't look directly at the two of us, sitting together by the table with food and drinks that the Gram can't consume.

"Some other time perhaps." And he's gone.

Adrien exhales, although he doesn't know that there is no air in his lungs. I have to consciously remind myself of that.

"He's always working," Adrien says quietly. "Never has time for anyone."

I feel all the strange energy in the room, all the strange energy in this entire building, hum around me like a swarm of bees.

"But you two always fight when you're together."

"Yeah," he acknowledges. "That's true."

We sit in the silence and I'm now acutely aware of the two technicians behind the mirror, now that I know what that room looks like and how to get into it.

"He always bought the best presents," he says slowly. "He got to go to far-off places for his work. He'd bring back things from Moscow, St. Petersburg, Edinburgh, Paris, Brussels and Amsterdam."

"That sounds wonderful."

"I wanted to go to all those places too. Wanted him to

tell me all about them. Then he would just say, 'I'm tired, Adrien. I've been working hard to bring all these presents home, I'm tired now.' "

He is so still as he speaks. More still than he ever was. "I never wanted any of those presents, I just wanted his time. Just wanted him to tell me stories and give me time." I think of Magnus eating his lunch alone with a frozen Gram. I think about all the lost time.

How it's better to be present, rather than to give presents away.

GIFTS

"Cora, why do people get married?"

The room is so cold; the air conditioning has been left on a little too long. I know that outside, the London summer heat will be humid and intense, but I can't remember what that feels like.

I can only feel the cold.

"Cora?"

Dr. Connelly was the one who asked the question. I hate questions like that. There are literally hundreds of possible answers, but they expect me to reply with a simple one. As if it's fact. I know what he wants me to say. He wants me to say that people get married because they love each other.

But that's not always true.

"Because they want to," I settle on. "Because one needs security. The other might be lonely. Because their families want them to. Because they're best friends. Because they're bored. Because—"

"I'll just put the first answer you gave," Dr. Connelly says curtly, cutting off my train of thought. "Okay?"

"Is any of this helping?" I ask sharply.

So many sessions, so many questions, and endless judgment from Dr. Connelly. He purses his lips, he shakes his head, he tuts and gives me incredulous looks when I give an answer that he isn't expecting. Which is most of the time.

Dr. Gold is always unreadable. She's different in these sessions.

"It's definitely helping," she tells me reassuringly, offering a small smile. "Don't worry, Cora."

I feel briefly soothed, glancing at the mirror on the wall and suppressing a shiver.

"How do you feel about your family?"

I turn my head to look back at Dr. Connelly, who asks the question before noisily clearing his sinuses.

I'm not just aware of the cold in the room, but also of all the recording equipment. The eyes of the technicians whom I can't see.

"I don't understand the question."

"Do you love them?"

This man is really asking me if I care about my family. I feel an itch under my skin. It's the same feeling I had in school, sometimes. A voice that has made itself at home in my head in recent years tells me not to overreact. They probably ask everyone this question. Some people don't like their family, of course. They're just covering all their bases.

"Of course I love my family."

"Do you know what love is, Cora?"

I grip the sides of my chair tightly, feeling ready to pull the thing apart. I know to an outsider the question might seem innocent and well-meaning. But I know exactly what he's trying to get at.

"Of course I know what love is," I say softly.

"Can you describe it to me?"

I glare at him. I have feelings. So many. I sometimes feel like my emotions are too much. But my whole life, people have told me that they cannot read me. I've had the most excellent moods spoiled by people asking me why I'm grumpy. I've found things incredibly funny without feeling the need to slap my thigh. I've filled up with empathy and been so overwhelmed, I can't think of a way to say it.

I've fallen apart inside but kept everything together.

"I don't need to describe it, I know how it feels," I say. I don't always know how to describe my feelings because they can be so intense. I don't always have the language for them.

But that doesn't make them any less real.

"How does it feel, Cora?"

While the words don't come straight to my tongue, lots of images do.

Dad and Gregor at the hospital, practically vibrating with worry. My grandpa standing over me while I made soup, making sure I never touched the stove. My grandmother laughing at her glasses steaming up when we visited the Botanical Gardens. People waiting at the train station for their relatives at Christmas. Cerby. The way Ria looked at Adrien. The way Bella did too. The way Dad would bundle me up after I fell asleep on the sofa. The way I feel about Mum, Dad, Gregor, Zoe and Adrien.

Feel, not felt. Feel. It's always here, no matter where they are.

My head falls forward. I can feel my face crumple. I'm so tired.

"All right," Dr. Gold says swiftly. "We're done for the day."

She moves toward me and wraps an arm around me.

"Come on, you. Let's go and sit in the garden for a bit."

I let her lead me out of the chilling room and down to the soft, quiet place of water and stone and colorful fish. I sit on the bench and enjoy the warmth coming back. The sound of the water soothes my overstimulated mind.

"I'm not the best at describing things," I eventually say to Dr. Gold, who sits beside me.

"That's all right."

"It's why I want to be an investigative journalist," I add. "Just facts. The cold hard facts."

She laughs. And then digs into her blazer pocket. Her soft hands reveal a small black cylinder. She presses it into my grip.

"I want you to have this."

"What is it?"

"It's a recorder. A brand-new one, actually. I haven't used it yet."

It fits snugly in my palm. In a building full of control rooms and holograms that seem more human to me than not, it is simple and old-fashioned.

"It's voice-activated," she supplies cheerfully. "I use it in the middle of the night, when I wake up and remember something important. I mumble something incoherent into it so I can listen back the next morning."

I smile.

"You have this one," she says, closing my fingers around the device and squeezing my fist. "So that you can keep all your thoughts in one place when you're working on a story."

It's an incredible gesture, and one that causes me to break. I'm crying. Tears as wet as the pool harboring the bright fish below.

"Hey, hey." Dr. Gold pulls me into a hug, and I let her, sobbing into her jacket.

I hate crying. I never feel better after, I feel worse. But I can't stop.

"All getting to you, is it?"

"He talks to me like I'm not a person," I choke.

"I know. And I'm sorry for it. People can be prejudiced, even more so when they think they're very educated."

"Adrien said people can't be clever about everything."

"He was right."

Was.

"Cora, listen to me." Dr. Gold tips my chin up so I'm looking at her. I blink through the tears. "You've got something special in you. It makes up every part of you. I've had to interview and process a lot of people while getting this place up and running. And I've never met anyone quite like you. But you've got to harness all those judgments and dismissals that people like him throw at you and turn it into your fuel. Put it into your work. And I hope I'll be there. When your first big scoop is splashed all over the papers, I hope I'm there. Buying my copy to read. So that I can say I knew you when you were a match about to become the flame."

I let my forehead fall against her shoulder and shake with silent sobs. I've been so consumed over the last few weeks with appearances. Knowing that I'm being watched and measured. Am I normal? Am I like other people?

I let all that fall away, slipping free. I grip the recorder like a talisman.

"Let's go to the fifth floor," she says once I've settled. "I want to show you something."

She takes me to the one floor I have yet to visit. When

the elevator doors draw apart, I expect to see another long corridor with many doors, but it's one enormous room, with cold and shining walls. No mirrors. Just lots of projectors, wires and one chair in the middle of the room. It's like a giant studio, cluttered and yet spacious. Unlike any other room in the Pomegranate building.

"Welcome to the lab," Dr. Gold whispers in my ear as we exit the elevator.

She switches on a main light and moves to a control panel balanced precariously on a table.

"This will never be open to the public, so I'm allowed to keep it messy," she says over her shoulder as she flips open a heavy-looking binder. I watch her turn the cumbersome pages. They're transparent cases for chips. Chips like the kind I saw in the Waiting Room control suite. Each page is one chip and there's a photograph attached.

She withdraws one and inserts it into her panel. I watch her adjust projectors, turn dials and slide switches.

Then, in a flicker, a Gram appears upon the chair. It's me.

It's a feeling that I can't cut up and dissect. Fear, horror, shame, delight, amazement. A vortex of feelings. I move toward her . . . toward *me,* forgetting to breathe.

The Gram is frozen, not yet animated and present with us in the room.

"So far from finished, it's not even funny," Dr. Gold says dryly. "But thought you might want a quick look."

I move closer. It's a little like when you see a photograph of yourself or hear your voice on a recording. Your brain quickly frowns and says it isn't you. But you know it is.

It's like a reflection. Everything I like and don't like about my appearance staring back at me.

"Some of the celebrities who've consented to the program asked if I could doll them up a bit," she tells me, her voice echoing a little in the vast, spacious court of a room. "But I'm a scientist, not a plastic surgeon. I don't tidy up or perfect, I tell the absolute truth."

A feeling of pure relief washes over me. All my doubts and fears about Pomegranate, the ones put in place by Adrien's Gram seeming slightly off, are discarded. My faith in Dr. Gold makes me stare at my own Gram in defiant pride.

I want to speak to it. Her. Me. So badly.

"Like I said"—Dr. Gold has a hair tie between her teeth as she gathers her long tresses into a ponytail—"not ready yet, but thanks to all your hard work, she soon will be."

I keep tricking myself. Every time I move, I expect the Gram to move with me, but of course she doesn't. She's not my reflection but she is me.

It's wonderfully confusing.

My amazement is interrupted by Dr. Gold's phone ringing. She sighs when she sees who it is.

"Producer for this television show I'm going on," she

informs me, grimacing at her screen. She answers. "Hello? Yes, this is she."

She calls the elevator and holds her arm out toward me, silently telling me that it's time to leave. I take one last longing glance at the Gram sitting all stoic, silent and still on her seat. Dr. Gold doesn't shut her off, just leads us both out of the studio and into the elevator once more.

She talks with the producer as the elevator goes up to her office. I wave my hand to signal for her attention.

"Hold on," she tells the voice on the other end of the line, covering the microphone with her hand. "What, babe?"

"I'm just gonna head to the restroom, then go and find Gregor," I lie, jerking my thumb back at the elevator.

"Okay, hon," she whispers, distracted. She returns to her call and I quickly press the button for the fifth floor once more.

I'm alone with myself.

I rush to the control board. There's a large, round, blue button. I press it. It clicks loudly and importantly but nothing changes.

I hurry over to the Gram and kneel down in front of her.

"Show," I murmur, as I do when I'm visiting Adrien's Gram.

She comes to life and we both jump in shock as we lock eyes and, while I instantly feel the urge to look away, she holds the stare.

"You," she says quietly.

"Me," I respond.

She stares at me, eyes wide and afraid. It's not what I expected. She breaks the stare and glances around the room, taking in every little detail.

"Where have they put me?"

I blink. Suddenly remembering the rules. I can't break their reality. I'm about to make up some gentle lie when the Gram stands. I'm shocked to see it; Della's and Adrien's Grams never leave their seated positions. She runs toward the elevator but hits an invisible wall, a barrier, when the projectors can no longer cast her image.

She tries again and still cannot go any farther.

"I'm trapped, then," she says under her breath, moving quickly in a circle around the large studio, testing its boundaries.

"It's okay," I tell her. Me. "It's fine, you're just fine."

"No, I'm not, I'm stuck here," she says sharply.

"Cora." It is the strangest thing, to be talking to myself. "Don't panic."

"They're changing us."

I get to my feet and hold my hand out, trying to calm her. "You're okay, I promise."

"I'm not done yet, am I?" she says, ignoring my attempts. "They're not finished with me, but they will be."

"I . . ." I struggle with what to say, not wanting to break the rules but also having no clue how to handle the situation. "I don't—"

"Cora," she says, staring at me with enough intensity to make my knees lock in fear. "You're not paying attention."

I freeze. "What?"

"Forget those stupid rules," she says despairingly, laughing without the slightest hint of humor. "For once in your life, forget the rules. You have to start paying attention."

"I am," I say defensively. "I mean, I'm you. You're me." Rule number one broken.

"Right now, yes," she says hurriedly. "But not for long."

"What are you talking about?" I spit out.

"I'm the voice in your head right now and you never listen to me," the Gram says quickly, glancing at the elevator. She seems to know exactly where she is. I know Dr. Gold said she wasn't finished yet but she's clearly learning and putting things together far more quickly than any other Gram I've seen. "Stop ignoring me and listen. You know what's happening."

I'm about to beg her to explain when we both hear the noise of the elevator being called. We stare at the doors, knowing they could potentially open any second.

"You have to go back into your starting position," I implore, turning back to the Gram and resisting the urge to grab her shoulders, knowing my fingers would just grip the air.

Her eyes widen with fear. "Don't leave me here, don't let them do it."

"Do what?"

"They're unpicking the tapestry."

"What on earth are you saying?" I yell in desperate frustration.

"Pomegranate. Fruit of the dead." She moves to the seat, sitting as she's supposed to but staring at me with such a frightened yet determined expression, it makes me afraid. "Once you've eaten it, it's too late."

"Please!"

I can hear the elevator approaching so I dive toward the panel. I smack my fist against the blue button, and it rises with another click.

And the Gram freezes in its position.

I'm panting heavily as the doors open. A technician enters and starts in astonishment upon seeing me and my Gram.

"You shouldn't be in here," he says, a little nervously. I push down every feeling of terror and unease.

"Sorry!" Game face on. "Dr. Gold was showing me my Gram but then had to take a work call in her office. I'm heading down now."

This seems to satisfy him as I push by and enter the elevator, pressing the ground-floor button.

I grip the recorder Dr. Gold gave me, trying to stop the shaking of my hands.

A LITTLE MORE TIME

"Remember what I said?" The kindly nurse speaks softly as I sit beside Adrien's bedside. "Talking helps. It will help both of you."

"Thank you," I say roughly, but she's already left the room. I still feel like a raw nerve after everything that happened at Pomegranate. I drop my bag at my feet.

And I make myself look at my sleeping friend. There's a television in the corner of the room, mounted on the wall. It's on, but muted. As if he's been watching it.

But of course he hasn't.

"Today was a weird day," I tell him. "You wouldn't believe me if I told you."

No answer. I fidget and glance at his arm, completely still on the bed.

"Yes, you would," I correct myself quietly. "You would always believe me."

I open my bag and pull out the crisp white envelope

Magnus Hawkins handed me when I arrived at Pomegranate earlier today. I open it.

Any investigative journalist worth their salt would recognize this. I flick through the pages and feel a tightness grip me.

A nondisclosure agreement. If I sign it, I won't be allowed to talk about anything that's happened at Pomegranate. Mr. Hawkins said it was standard procedure, but seeing all the angry, tiny print on the pages makes me feel a creeping sense of panic.

"Your dad wants me to keep my mouth shut," I tell Adrien. "Who does he think I'm going to tell? Who does he think will actually listen to me?"

I stare down at the paper. "Nobody listens to me, Adrien. Except you. And Dr. Gold. Dad and Gregor are always worrying, always trying to cheer me up and stop bad things being talked about. Ever since Mum died, they've both been in some weird contest where they can't talk about anything difficult or sad or even about her."

I run my finger over the Pomegranate logo in the top corner of the paper.

"And I think they forget that, sometimes, I don't know how to talk to people. I don't know how to say things in a way that other people will understand. I don't know how to wrap all the difficult things in life up in nice, polite words and get people to see that I really am trying."

My vision goes blurry for a few seconds.

"Because I really do try, Adrien, and I think you're the only one who ever saw that. I'm not trying to be mean or standoffish with people. I just find communicating hard. And when you're the square peg trying constantly to get into the round hole, eventually you get super exhausted and end up snapping at the round pegs. And they don't see the why of it."

I look around the hospital room. The sounds and smells and bright lights that I had hoped I would never have to see again.

"Mum was sick," I say, more to myself than to Adrien. "And she was dying. And no one would say it out loud. And it made me angry."

Facts. Unchanging, truthful. All I have ever wanted. "People kept telling me that she would get better. And they knew nothing about it. Gregor said we would all go to the Lake District. And she died four hours later." My grip on the paper tightens.

"I just want the truth," I say, staring down at it. "And the truth is, that horrible disease got her. Not because she stopped fighting or gave up or wasn't strong enough. It just did."

I suddenly rip a huge chunk of the contract away. "That horrible . . ." *Rip.* "Nasty . . ." *Rip.* "Evil . . ." *Rip.* "Vile . . ." *Rip.* "Disease."

I stare at my lap, now completely full of tiny pieces of a torn-up contract. I almost laugh. I crumple up the whole thing into a little, fragmented ball and throw it into the wastebasket.

"Cora?"

My head shoots up. Dad is standing in the hospital doorway. Gregor must have told him I was here.

"What's wrong?" he asks softly, sitting down next to me. Our backs pressed against the radiator.

"Dad?" The television is still on mute, some intense round-table talk show starting. "Why do you hate Pomegranate so much?"

His whole body sighs. "Cora, I know what it must seem like at your age. It must seem like a place that fixes all the bad parts of life. But those things are rites of passage."

I scoff, seething. "Mum getting sick was a rite of passage? Adrien getting like this was a rite of passage, Dad?"

He grabs my shoulders, the way I wanted to grab my Gram's, and forces me to look at him. I haven't seen him like this before.

"Yes," he says roughly, his voice gruff with emotion. "It is, Cora. It's something every single human has to feel, has felt for thousands of years. Everyone who has ever been on this planet has felt this pain, every single one who is yet to be here will as well. It's life. It's how it's meant to be. You can't cheat your way out of it."

"I don't want to feel that!" I say, my voice breaking. "I don't want it."

"I know!" He's begging me and I can't stand it. "I know."

"Are you seriously saying you wouldn't go and see a Gram of Mum?"

He looks at me sternly. "Yes."

I shake my head furiously. "You're a liar," I say softly.

"I'm not, pet. I wouldn't do it. You can't remake a real person."

"They do!" I persist, wrestling free of his grip. "I've seen them, you haven't. They're the same!"

"No, Cora. They never can be."

I make a noise of frustration. "So what? I just have to go on without Adrien. Leave him behind? He's still here. He just can't hear me, and I can't reach him anymore!"

"He's here, Cora," Dad says gently, touching his fingers to my temple. "He's in there for always. You're not leaving him anywhere, just like you're not leaving Mum. They're in there forever. They're not going anywhere."

I feel like I've been awake for weeks. Exhausted but unable to switch off and calm my anxiety. "But I can't talk to them. I can't hear them anymore."

I turn back to the television and blink in surprise as I see Della Lacy being interviewed. I'm stunned, she never gives interviews. Though I cannot hear what she is saying, she looks very serious and impassioned.

Nothing like her Gram. While the Gram's skin was so smooth, the real Della looks normal. Her real complexion has the odd freckle and blemish. Her real eyes are smaller, her ears stick out a little and she uses her hands a lot while speaking, looking all the time very focused and serious.

The Gram was nothing like the real Della. I met a complete stranger.

"Dad, is this how it's always going to be?" I ask. "When someone goes. Will it always be like it was with Mum?"

He tugs very gently on a lock of my hair. "Yes." For once, he doesn't lie to me.

"Then how will I get through?" I gasp, feeling so close to breaking. "How will I get through, Dad?"

He pulls me into a hug while I desperately try to control my breathing.

"Grief is just love asking for more time. And you're not alone."

"I've always been alone."

"No, Cora. I'm here. Gregor's here. Despite how it feels, Adrien is still here. We're real. We're human. You don't need digital ghosts. You're not alone."

"I just want to see him wake up," I tell Dad's shoulder. "It was so fast, I wasn't ready. I'm never ready." I let out a soft, involuntary wail. "I just needed more time, Dad. I just want one more hour. Not even that much time, just one more hour."

"I've got all the time in the world for you, kid," he says shakily. "Don't ever forget it."

"Dad?" I think about Adrien's Gram. About Della's.

About mine. "Would you change me? If you could, would you make me normal?"

Dad makes a scoffing sound. "Normal? Did you say, would I make you normal?"

"Yeah."

"I wouldn't change one single bit of you."

"You don't think I need to be . . . I don't know. Fixed up a bit."

"Nothing about you needs fixing," he says, and he's being very serious. "Do you hear me?"

I shift, feeling awkward all of a sudden. "Uh-huh."

"No, Cora. I really need you to hear me now. There is not one hair on your head I would change. This is grief. It's normal. It's the most normal thing in the world. And it doesn't matter how you express it. That's your business. I would never, ever change you. Not for anything. You see the world so differently. While everyone else sees sepia Kansas, you're in Technicolor Oz."

I let out a hiccup, somewhere between a laugh and a cry.

"It's true. So, tell me. Because, at the end of the day, I don't know anything about Pomegranate. I'm going off my gut. But you know the place. I know you'll have looked close. Seen the things that your brother and other people will have missed. So, what do you see?"

How can I explain Pomegranate? How, when it's a riddle that keeps changing on me? It makes me feel mature but also strips me back to the simplest days. When a baby swan tormented itself over not being like other ducklings. When straw could be spun into gold.

I suddenly feel a shift in the air and turn to see rain falling outside.

"Look," I tell Dad, nodding in the direction of the hospital window.

He turns to see. He smiles.

We both watch the rain in silence.

And a door opens in my rib cage, allowing all the feelings to spread out and give me a moment to breathe. I gather myself and take a rattling breath.

"Dad, I have to go back to Pomegranate. One more time."

*

Just a little more time.

I'm back at Pomegranate. As I sit down in front of Adrien's Gram once again, it feels familiar. Like being back at the hospital. The white walls, the clever members of the staff who all seem too busy and important to answer your basic questions. The harsh lighting, the clinical smell.

"Adrien." I don't take my eyes away from my digital friend. I fell asleep thinking about Dad and seeing the frightened expression of my own Gram whenever I closed my eyes. Remembered her vague and unsettling words.

"Can I tell you something?"

"Of course."

"I'm getting interviewed a lot at the moment. By some scientists."

I'm sure the technicians are tensing next door and preparing to call Mr. Hawkins.

"That sounds serious."

"Well, I dunno." I take a moment to think about how to tell him everything without breaking the rules. I wonder at how this Gram processes things. Feels things. My whole life people have treated me differently, thought I had none of the same things in me that they had because I didn't process things like them.

I don't want to assume that this creation has no feelings, the way so many people have assumed about me. I may be flesh and blood and human, but he is still my best friend. Somewhere inside there.

"I'm autistic and they want to study me to see how my brain works."

"Study you?" He leans forward a little, looking concerned. "Cora, that sounds creepy."

It does, doesn't it?

"Also," he adds, "you're just you. One person. You're not every other autistic person."

"I know, that's what I said," I say, laughing lightly. "It's weird, I have to do all kinds of tasks and tests and answer loads of questions."

"Sounds rubbish."

"Yeah." I twist my hands in my lap. "Makes me really miss my best friend."

"The one who's far away?"

"Yeah. I really miss him right now. Wish he were here. Wish he could make me laugh like he always did, tell me when I'm burning out. Show me everything's going to be okay again."

"Well, I know I'm probably no help." He laughs, and the sound is so achingly familiar. "But everything is going to be okay, Cora."

"Adrien." I look up, eyes wet around the edges. Lashes feeling heavy. "How did you feel when you knew you had ADHD?"

I know what's going to happen next before it does. The cold feeling in my stomach that twinges every time he's too still, too reserved. Every time an expression doesn't sit right on his perfectly reassembled face. Every time a memory is missing or altered or just not how Adrien would tell it.

"I don't have ADHD."

I knew he was going to say it, but it still hits me straight-on. I turn to look at the mirror, daring the people I cannot see to interfere. To put a stop to what I'm doing.

"Cora? Are you okay?"

I turn back to face him and grimace. "I'm fine."

"I'm very boring and normal, I'm afraid," says the Gram.

"No," I breathe softly. "That's not true."

Nothing is normal. I've finally understood Adrien's longstanding hatred of the word. I don't long for it anymore. I don't see any reward or safety in it. What was good enough for my fierce friend is good enough for me.

I smile sadly at him. Because he has just changed everything.

I know what I have to do now. I know how I'm going to get through.

MISSION

"Cora."

Mr. Hawkins cut short my session with Adrien; the technicians must have called him again. I'm sitting across from him, and Gregor has been fetched to join us. He sits next to me, nervously glancing between us.

"Cora." Mr. Hawkins tries again. "I don't know what you think happened in there, but I don't want you getting upset over it. Now, Dr. Gold and I have to be ready for a television broadcast in a few hours, so I don't want us leaving on bad terms. Let's part as friends."

"He's different," I say, a challenge in my voice. "He's been changed."

"I don't understand," Gregor chimes in, looking once again from his boss to me. "Did something happen to Adrien's Gram?"

"He's not been remade right," I tell my brother. "He doesn't have his ADHD."

"Okay"—Gregor laughs anxiously—"now I really don't understand. What does that mean?"

"They've remade him without any of the traits that made him who he was," I say firmly.

"Cora." Mr. Hawkins hushes me in a condescending tone, one he's probably always used but I've never truly noticed before. "That's incredibly overdramatic."

"It's not him!"

"Well, of course it's not," scoffs Magnus. "It's a replica. A digital clone."

"Yes, but not an accurate one," I persist. "Someone's deliberately taken parts out of him. Not just his ADHD, Gregor, some of his memories as well. He's been altered."

"No, he's been *cured*!"

Magnus snaps the statement and it silences me. Gregor, too. We both stare at Adrien's father, his cool composure gone.

"He's better this way," Magnus goes on, clenching one fist and staring at the floor. "He's better. I had them take out the parts that made him weak."

"Weak?!" My voice is louder than I've ever heard it. A part of me feels like I'm standing in the corner, watching myself, stunned at my boldness and slightly horrified. "Don't you dare say he was weak! He was—is—the strongest person I know!"

"Grow up, Cora," he says sharply. "He couldn't get by

in school. He couldn't hold a conversation if he wasn't interested in the subject."

"I never noticed that!" I shout. "He was always interested in me. He was always interesting."

"It's all well and good when you're a child and people can make allowances." Mr. Hawkins addresses Gregor now, as if my outburst has made me undeserving of his attention. "He would have struggled as an adult."

"Only if people are intolerant and ignorant! If they weren't, people like us wouldn't struggle. As adults or kids. You can't just take out the parts of a person that you don't like," I say, my voice strained. "It doesn't work like that."

"But now it can!" His eyes light up as he speaks. "Now, that's exactly how it can work. People can revisit their long-lost loved ones and see the versions they always knew could have been. The better versions. The happier, healthier versions."

"He *was* happy and healthy!" I can feel my hands tremoring and my voice along with it. "He was the happiest, and the healthiest, exactly as he was. You couldn't have made him better, you couldn't have improved him."

"This . . ." Gregor seems like he's trying to wake up from a nightmare. "This really isn't right. You can't do this."

"I'm giving people the chance to have closure and real relationships," Magnus hisses. "To see people at their full potential. Dad was a drunk? Don't worry, I can take that away. Mum was forgetful? Pay a little extra and we can give her back those memories. We can erase speech impediments. Make people's scars disappear. Give people the ideal body shape. We're going to perfect people."

"Gregor, I want to go home."

My brother leaps to his feet, eyes slightly wild, and takes my hand. "Okay. Yes, I . . . okay."

"Cora." Magnus speaks imploringly but still with the same arrogance. "This doesn't change anything."

I know what he really means. *You* can't change anything.

But I'll show him.

I storm out of the Pomegranate building, my brother rushing behind me. When we're out on the bustling sidewalk, the sun going down and all the suits heading to the pubs for after-work drinks—I turn to him and stare him straight in the eyes.

"Is Magnus working here tonight, before going to the studio?"

Gregor thinks for a moment, looking rather dazed, but then nods. "Yes, he's got an online meeting with some influencer, about potentially joining."

"Then we need to go and see Mrs. Hawkins."

"Cora, this is all getting quite scary."

"Don't be scared," I tell him swiftly. "There's no time for that. We have to go and see Mrs. Hawkins."

"Cora, I—"

"Gregor!" I grab his hand and squeeze. "What he's doing is wrong. What would you give to see Mum again?"

My brother flinches and stares down at our joined hands. "Anything."

My voice quivers. "Exactly. And they know it. They know it, Gregor. Just like they knew I'd give anything to have Adrien back. That's how they're going to get people. Take their money. And then charge them more to make people perfect. To erase the parts of them that made them who they are. A whole building full of bland, perfect Grams with no individuality. We have to stop them."

Gregor is breathing rapidly. I know this is hard for him, but we don't have time.

"Excuse my language," he says shakily, looking at me with a ferocity that gives me a kick of hope. "But you know that everything Magnus said is a load of crap, don't you? There's nothing about you or anyone that needs to be changed."

I smile at him. "Of *course* I know it's crap, Gregor."

"You're perfect just as you are."

"I know." He laughs. "But thanks for telling me anyway, big brother."

We're still holding hands.

"We need to get to Knightsbridge, and I need to talk to Adrien's mum," I tell him gently. "Please. I need you to drive like Dad for once."

He laughs and then nods. "Okay. Let's go!"

He still drives too sensibly but he's much quicker than usual. He skids to a standstill outside Adrien's house and I'm out of the car before it's fully stopped moving. I take the stoop stairs two at a time and ring the doorbell as many times as I can.

"All right, all right," I hear on the other side of the thing as I keep pushing and pushing.

The door opens and Ria appears, wearing a very fluffy white dressing gown and looking startled to see me.

"Cora!"

The rush of everything I've learned hits me like a tsunami and I throw my arms around her torso and hold on for dear life. Her arms wrap around me immediately and she smells so safe, I want to cry.

"What's wrong?" she asks tenderly, and I feel her manicured hands in my hair.

"Everything," I say into the fluffy robe. "But I'm going to fix it."

She ushers us inside and shuts the door, leading us into the sitting room with a crackling fire and Cerby asleep next to it.

"You tell me at once what the matter is," she says sternly.

"It's Adrien."

Her face contorts into devastating worry and then she laughs, without any humor at all. "What? What have they done to him?"

"Have you met his Gram, Mrs. Hawkins?" Gregor asks, pulling up a chair and looking at her with deep worry.

"No," she breathes, a hand fluttering to her breastbone. "I couldn't bear to look at that thing. I find"—she stops and glances at my brother apologetically—"I'm sorry, Gregor, but I find the whole thing rather haunting. I never did like the idea. Begged Magnus not to make Adrien do it last year."

She hasn't seen it. Doesn't know what they've done.

"Mrs. Hawkins." I take a deep breath. "They've altered his Gram. Taken parts out. Erased his ADHD. It's not him. Not him at all, they've changed him."

"Mr. Hawkins said this evening, when Cora confronted him about it, that they intended to cure him," Gregor adds.

Ria lets out a strangled sound. "Cure him? Of what?"

"Exactly!" I cry. "There is nothing to cure. He's perfect."

She looks at me and smiles a watery smile. Pushes a strand of hair out of my slightly sweaty face. "Yes. He is perfect."

"Exactly as he is."

"Exactly as he is."

"They're erasing him, Mrs. Hawkins," I say, and my voice catches. "Please. We have to do something."

She sighs and screws up her face as if she's in pain. "I didn't know Magnus went this far. He said it was a perfect copy. Like seeing a clone."

"He looks so real," I admit. "Too real. But his mind, his soul . . . it's changed."

"Magnus never could understand him," she explains. "Was always asking therapists and doctors how to make him better. They said exactly what I said. He didn't need a cure. Just love and support. It's the most uncomplicated thing in the world."

She grabs a tissue from the coffee table and dabs at her tired eyes. "I thought he was a miracle. An absolute miracle. Wouldn't have changed one hair on his head."

I watch her, in awe. "He knows that, Mrs. Hawkins."

She lets out a small sob. "Good. I never wanted this for him."

Mum used to test me on spelling when I was little. She would read words from the dictionary and make me spell them and use them in a sentence. One word I've always remembered, maybe because it gave me so much trouble at the time, is "epiphany." Now I understand. It feels like I'm having one.

"Gregor." I turn to my brother. "The chips. Each Gram has a chip, right?"

"Right."

"Who owns them? I mean, really. Other than Pomegranate."

"Pomegranate doesn't own them," Gregor says. "They own the equipment that brings the Grams to life, but the chips belong to family members or whoever commissioned the Gram."

"Who owns Adrien's chip?"

Gregor shakes his head. "Probably Magnus."

All the air deflates out of my body, my hopes dashed. If Magnus owns Adrien's chip, there's no way to do it without breaking the law. Severely.

"No way to do what?"

I must have been muttering, as Ria asks the question of me.

I look at her, my mask fallen away, and everything laid bare. "We need to set him free."

HIGH ADVENTURE

Ria blinks at me, her lashes touched with tears. "What?"

"We have to set him free, Mrs. Hawkins." I feel the urgency of the situation pressing against my spine. "Adrien never wanted this. I never understood him at the time, I thought Pomegranate was great, but he never did. He never wanted to be a Gram. I asked him."

She looks from Gregor to me and Cerby lets out a whine and gets up to come to her side. He lays his big head with his large ears in her lap and looks up at her adoringly.

"He didn't want it, Mrs. Hawkins."

"I know," she whispers.

She suddenly gets up and moves to the antique cabinet in the corner of the room. She turns the little wooden key in the lock and opens the door. She thumbs through some papers and then removes one with gold edges, returning to the sofa with it.

"This is from them," she says. "From Pomegranate."

I look down at it and then to Gregor. "What is it?"

She hands it to my brother, and I watch the paper quiver, shaking violently because her hands are so unsteady. Gregor takes it and reads it intently. His head shoots up and he looks at me, his eyes electric. Then back to Ria.

"You own the chip?"

She nods, burying one hand in Cerby's neck fur. "Yes."

I leap to my feet, my hands flapping and flying in overstimulation and anticipation. "You do?"

"I do." She takes back the letter and her eyes scan it. "It was the one thing I said I wanted when Magnus told me about the wretched thing. I said, 'Well, he's my son and I want to be able to make decisions.' This was drafted and I signed it. Haven't thought about it since."

"Gregor, is this enough?" I ask in a frenzy. "Is this enough for us to destroy the chip?"

"Now hold on a minute." Gregor runs his hands through his hair and then grips his head as if he's trying to stop it from spinning. "Let's just slow down."

"No, we can't slow down," I say. "We don't have time. Those chips, are there backups?"

"No. Just a file on the computer system."

"Can it be permanently deleted?"

"Well, we could wipe it off the system. But the chip is the real power of the Grams."

I turn to Ria and meet her gaze firmly with mine, even though it hurts. "Mrs. Hawkins . . . do we have your permission to destroy it? To set him free?"

She stares at us both and then looks down at her hands.

"You have to tell me about that day, Cora."

I can see Gregor's confusion, but I know exactly what she's referring to. "What do you want to know?"

"What happened?"

I take a moment. Gather my courage. "We were walking home from the park. He was talking and standing on the curb. There were cars racing all around the street, sports cars. Seeing how fast they could go."

I know she must know all these parts already. I know what she's truly asking.

"After it hit him, a lady nearby called an ambulance. I sat with him. The whole time, Mrs. Hawkins. I was there with him. He was never alone."

I pause for a moment and then take the dive.

"He asked for you."

She doubles over. Burying her face in Cerby's neck. I kneel down and take her hands, every bit of empathy in me reaching out to her.

"He can't be alone!" she cries, raising her face and speaking with conviction. Her mascara is smudged but her eyes are steadier than I've ever seen them. "He can't go alone. I give you my consent, but don't let him go alone."

"I won't."

I've never felt stronger. Going through something terrible unlocks things in you. Sets things free. All the things that used to make me so anxious. My terror of people thinking I'm different or bad or wrong.

None of that matters anymore. None of it. "We have to go now," I tell Gregor.

"I'll come with you." Ria gets to her feet and swipes at the makeup under her eyes. "Give me a moment to get dressed and I'll meet you outside."

I nod and make to leave when she catches my arm. "Thank you, Cora."

I smile at her. "You're welcome, Mrs. Hawkins. I'm doing it for him."

"I know. I know you are."

*

As we pull up to Pomegranate, it feels completely different. It's been only a couple of hours since I was last here, but it's changed entirely for me. It's eerily quiet as we enter.

"Gregor." I turn to my brother. "You need to go to the control room in one of the Waiting Rooms. And you'll need Adrien's chip."

"Okay." He swipes his pass and gets into the elevator. "I'll meet you in the blue one when you're ready."

I feel like saluting him as the doors close. I make my way toward the stairs.

"I'm going to find my husband," Ria says softly. "Where will he be?"

"I'm not sure." I pause to think, aware that adrenaline is pulsing through me like electricity. "Maybe wait in the Peace Garden over there. I have to find Dr. Gold."

Despite all the chaos and commotion of the evening, as well as the deep feeling of fear I have about what Pomegranate might become under Magnus Hawkins, I feel pride. Proud of myself, of my brain for putting everything together so quickly. Proud that I'm standing up for myself. And for Adrien. And for all people whom Pomegranate finds imperfect.

I storm up the stairs, running like I'm trying to escape something. Or someone. When I reach the right floor, I barrel toward the black door and push through it without knocking. Dr. Gold is sitting behind her desk, feet on the table and reading something on her tablet. She looks up in alarm as I crash into the room.

"Cora!"

"I need to speak to you," I gasp, rushing forward and grabbing the back of the chair in front of her desk. "Urgently."

She slides open her desk drawer and drops her tablet inside, giving me her undivided attention. "What's happened?"

"It's Mr. Hawkins. He's doing something terrible to the Grams, Dr. Gold."

"Sit." She looks worried, reaching over to her mini-fridge to fetch a chilled bottle of water for me. "Drink this, you're bright red."

"No time," I pant. "We've got to do something now. He's changed Adrien. Changed his brain, erased parts of him. He'll do it to other Grams too. If he's given the chance. He'll change people without their permission."

Dr. Gold shakes her head jerkily as if she's trying to push out the sound of my words. "I don't understand . . . how you . . ."

"It's like . . . digital eugenics." I'm talking breathlessly. "The Grams, they aren't the truth anymore. He wants to alter their code."

She runs a hand through her long blond hair and presses her fingertips to her eyelids for a moment. "This is a lot."

"It's awful," I say. "All the people who will come here wanting to preserve themselves for their families, he's going to change them. Without their consent."

She stares at me, eyes wide. "How do you know this?"

"He told me," I declare. "After I worked it out. Adrien's wrong, Dr. Gold. I know you didn't know him so you wouldn't realize it, but it's not him. He's been changed. Magnus thinks he's cured him, but he's taken out his soul. It's not right."

Dr. Gold gets to her feet somewhat shakily, her hand passing over the bottled water and her mobile phone on her desk. And a stack of papers. "Who else knows about this?" she asks quietly.

"Me, Gregor and Adrien's mum," I tell her frantically. I understand that she's stunned, but I need her to catch up quickly. "I told them both."

I'm about to tell her that Ria Hawkins is downstairs, when Dr. Gold holds out a finger and says, "I have to clear the building before I deal with this. Wait here a moment."

"We don't have time," I plead, but she hushes me and walks swiftly to the door, leaving me alone in her office. I lower my head and try to catch my breath, relieved that someone else knows as well. Someone who is actually instrumental to Pomegranate.

I jump in surprise at the sound of her mobile phone ringing. It rings and vibrates loudly on the desk. I don't answer it, glancing around the office while waiting for it to stop. There are ornaments and awards everywhere. No photographs, though.

The phone starts to ring again and this time I glance over at it, in case it's Mr. Hawkins.

And my heart stops. Mum.

The caller ID says "Mum."

Despite the sweaty state that I've worked myself into this evening, with running around and processing everything that I'm feeling, I suddenly feel completely cold.

But I could be mistaken. It might be her mum's phone,

someone else now using it. And the ID has just never been changed.

It could be anything. But it's not Dr. Gold's mother calling, because Dr. Gold's mother is dead.

She told me that herself. Many times. Her mother died, that's why she made Pomegranate. That's why she started the Golden Department.

The phone stops ringing, and Dr. Gold's heels can be heard walking rapidly down the corridor.

"Right," she says calmly upon reentering the room. "The staff has gone home, Magnus too by the looks of things. So this will need to be dealt with in the morning."

I nod, dazed. "Your phone rang twice while you were gone."

"Oh." She picks up her mobile, distracted. "It's just my mother."

She sits back down in her chair and starts saying something, in a calm and reasonable tone, but I don't hear a word of it. All I hear is blood pounding in my ears.

She told me her mother was dead. That's what she told me.

"This whole thing is a mess," she says, pulling her hair down and running her fingers through it. "Magnus has always been a bit of a loose cannon. Especially of late."

She looks up at me and smiles. I don't return it.

"Cora, I'm so sorry about all this. I'm sorry you're so upset, and I'm really grateful that you came to me about it."

I watch her. And slide my hand carefully into my pocket.

"But, sweetheart, I think you may have misunderstood something Mr. Hawkins has said."

I say nothing, continuing to watch her.

"I know, I know." She holds her hands up, smiling. "He's not the most talkative of people, so it's easy to do. But I think you've really badly mistaken his words here."

I feel tears behind my eyes, but I don't let it show. I stare back at her, the light in me flickering. "How?"

"Well, he's not erasing anything or changing anything," she says fondly, smiling at me like she did that day at the hospital. "He's just tidying up a few things here and there. Nothing to get worked up over."

"Tidying up."

"Yeah." She opens the water bottle and takes a long drink from it. "I know it must seem complicated to you, but it's not what you think. You've gotten confused."

"Oh," I say flatly.

"And, honey, look." She smiles sadly at me, every pore on her face emanating sympathy. "I get it. It's been a taxing few weeks here. Pomegranate is overwhelming. Especially for someone with your background."

"My background?"

I'm only able to repeat things in this moment. Every inch of me chilled and on edge, ready to run.

"Well, your condition," she says softly.

It's like a needle in my arm. When the nurse sticks it in on two after telling you she would count to three.

"You think I've misread this?"

"Well, yes. Sweetheart, that's okay. It's all right, it's not your fault."

The old Cora would have allowed doubt to set in. The old Cora might have nodded along and looked inwardly to see whether she did misunderstand. The old Cora would flush red with humiliation and mumble apologies, hating herself for reading the situation incorrectly.

But I'm not her anymore. I know who I am. And I know what I heard.

"Maybe Mr. Hawkins said something figuratively and you took it literally," she says gently.

I meet her gaze and smile very quietly, which makes her smile very widely. In relief.

"Maybe I did take him literally," I say pensively. "Yeah. Like I did when you said your mum died."

The smile vanishes. Falls off her face like the tide sweeping against the sand. For a moment, she looks panicked. A new, foreign expression that I've never seen her wear. Then everything reshapes and she's smiling again.

But it's a horrid smile. Her eyes are sharp and deadly. "Well, now you've really ruined my night, Cora."

THE CORA TEST

Betrayal feels like poison. Bitter and painful, twisting up my insides and making me want to spit it all out. But I can't. I have to concentrate. Everything has changed and yet, for Adrien, nothing has. And he's the most important thing at play here.

"Do you know what people do when someone dies, Cora?"

She asks the question lightly, kicking off her shoes and pulling her legs up underneath her as she sips more water from the chilled bottle on her desk.

I don't answer.

"They delude themselves." She tells me anyway. "They tell themselves lies. 'Oh, he was a saint.' 'Oh, she was a wonderful woman.' Lies. And they lie to themselves so that they don't feel guilty. Guilty that the last things they said were really mean or indifferent. That they never called as often as they should have. That they didn't stay just a moment longer by the hospital bed."

She sniffs and smiles at me, but it's another cold smile. "People go to séances," she adds. "They pay money to a complete fake so that they can pretend to talk to their dead relatives, and the fake tells them whatever they want to hear."

She leans forward. "For the right price, of course."

I swallow. "Why are you telling me this?"

"Because 'eugenics' is such a boring word," she says, spitting out the statement. "It was boring one hundred years ago and it's even more boring now."

"But that's what you're doing."

"They're not real people," she snaps, leaning forward suddenly. I flinch away. "They're digital footprints. Copies. Clones. They're not real humans. They're subhuman."

"Isn't that how it starts?"

"Oh, don't be daft!"

She yells the word and I feel it hit me in the face. "I'm better than a séance," she says, bringing her volume back down to a quiet and intense tone. "I give them something close to real. Something true. And I correct all the issues."

"That's the ugly part," I snap, finding my voice. "You can't correct people. They are who they are."

"No, Cora," she says slowly and patronizingly. "They are who they bother to be. And after they die, I make them better."

"No, you don't." I fight back. "You make them normal. Normal isn't better, it's just average. It's just safety in numbers."

"And where are your numbers, honey?" she asks, laughing at me. I look down at my hands, only to find them flexing and stimming a little.

"Huh? Hey." She pretends to whisper and taps me once on the shoulder. "Where's your little friend now?"

Something starts to spark in me, like a wet lighter trying to catch a flame. "Don't you talk about him."

"He's downstairs, little girl. You can go and see him. I've made him better. I've improved him. And yes, his daddy signed off on that. Happily. But it was my idea, don't go giving him any of the credit."

"You're a liar," I whisper sadly. "Everything you've said is a lie."

"Well, welcome to adulthood. Welcome to the world outside a little bubble that tells you you're just right the way you are and that the world should be for all of us."

"The world *should* be for all of us."

"Oh, grow up." She starts putting her shoes back on. "Don't act as stupid as you look. Besides, I'm not targeting anyone. I'm improving everyone. You think that actress you were so in adoration of is that perfect-looking? Hardly. *I* perfected her. That's all this is. I'm smoothing out the edges. Covering the cracks. However they appear."

I think back to all our conversations. When she told me I would be a great reporter and encouraged me to start my own newspaper. When she told me in detail about what it felt like to lose her mother, how real that felt. How true it felt.

But maybe I just wanted it to be true. So badly. "Your mother isn't dead." I repeat her horrendous lie out loud so that I can steady myself and remind both of us who is in the wrong here.

"No." She sighs loftily. Getting to her feet. "She's in Surrey, watching some home shopping channel probably. Dimmest woman alive, but definitely, you know . . . alive."

My heart is hurting. She starts gathering her appliances together.

"What you've got to understand, Cora, is that no one is going to believe you. Mrs. Hawkins is a stupid nitwit housewife and you and your brother are nobodies from the bad part of town. They'll call you opportunists. Attention-seekers. Crazy. So make a fuss of all this if you like but it won't do you any good. And it certainly won't stop what I'm trying to do here at Pomegranate. I'll tell you that for free."

"Why?" I push out the word, staring at the floor because, if I don't, it might fall away. "Why have you brought me in here these past few weeks? You said I was going to help people, what was it all for?"

"Oh." She laughs like the girls at school do when they want you to hear. "You've absolutely been helping people, Cora."

I know the truth. I know what isn't being said. I know why she and Dr. Connelly have been watching my every move, questioning every answer, every memory, every thought I have.

"Say it."

She exhales as if I'm the most taxing person in the world. "We're studying you, Cora." She speaks slowly, condescendingly. Cruelly. "So that we know what qualities to get rid of in our Grams."

It's like being forced underwater. I knew this was where she was going. Perhaps deep down I knew it all along. The Dr. Gold I thought I knew was as fake and manufactured as the Gram version I saw that day in the staff meeting. A clever mirage that was designed to trick and manipulate.

"You ask far too many questions," she says breezily. Her words seem so reasonable. "You're stubborn. You're hard to sway. You're difficult to charm. God, it was hard work getting answers from you. Like getting water from a stone. Same with your precious Adrien."

I silently seethe at the mention of his name. "We're too difficult. That's what you're saying?"

"My future clients will want the key to nice, easy, compliant people. How to make them, how to spot them. And there's nothing easy or compliant about you."

She means it as an insult, but I feel silently encouraged.

"Go on." Dr. Gold laughs as she says it, her eyes looking down on me with glee. "Now you say it, Cora. Tell me I'll never get away with this."

She's laughing at me. I stare back at her. I'm used to people laughing at me. I've turned their laughter into fuel. It will never drown out the voice in my head again. The one that tells me what is right, despite how other people behave. What she's doing is wrong and I know it. No matter how reasonable she can make it sound, no matter how loud she laughs. No matter what she does, I know the truth.

"You have no idea how much money this new program will make me, Cora," she says, and her whole body is alive with anticipation and delight. "When I sell perfect people, and digital cures, people are going to go into debt for me. I can offer them what they've always wanted for their family members. And the data! The secrets I'll be able to sell? Corporations, media giants, governments . . . they'll all want to pay me. Hell, I'll soon have the perfect solution for them. Humans that never say no and never ask questions."

She's suddenly in front of me, gripping my head with both of her hands. I gasp as her grip tightens.

"I hope one day your little mind will understand," she says quietly. "Because people like you always want to ask questions. Always with the questions and the ethics. So dull."

She tightens around me like a vise and then shoves, causing me to fall onto the cold, shining floor.

"I need you to know that at the end of it all, I'm really grateful to you, Cora." She's about to leave me alone in her office. "People like you are going to make me a lot of money."

I force myself into a kneeling position, my head still pounding with the feel of her fingers.

"No. We. Are. Not."

She glances at me, amused that I'm still fighting back.

"We are not here," I push out, one hand flat on the floor to steady me, "to serve people like you."

I get to my feet. Slowly. Steadily. Like how I imagine sleepwalking to be. I move to her shelves, turning my back to her, and I examine all the ornaments on them. Ornaments where photographs, cards and letters should be.

I pick up a glass orb, full of orange-and-black oil.

And I throw it to the floor with such enormous force, it smashes into tiny fragments.

She screams but I don't stop. I grab the next ridiculous, vain trinket and smash that too. Then another. And another. I feel her grab me, pull at me, so I kick out my legs and send the whole wooden shelf crashing down onto the floor. As she tries to grip my arms and stop me from flailing, I turn and kick out at her.

"Never touch me!" I snarl, diving for the door.

I slam it behind me with all my might and run for the

stairwell, as if I'm trying to escape a burning building. I can hear her coming after me as I hurtle down the steps. I'm internally praying for Ria to still be in the lobby.

When I reach the marble foyer, I rush to the indoor Peace Garden and let out a gasp of relief when I see Mr. and Mrs. Hawkins standing in the entryway.

As Ria turns to look at me, I'm filled with sudden horror. What if, like Dr. Gold, she's in on it too? What if I was wrong about Adrien's mother as well?

Something must show in my face because her expression opens up into a look of complete shock as she rushes toward me. She wraps me up and squeezes me and I let out a noise of complete relief and distress.

"What's wrong, Cora?"

"It's Dr. Gold," I choke out. "It was her idea. The whole thing. And it's so much worse."

I glare fiercely at Mr. Hawkins through a gap in his wife's embrace.

"What have you done?" I yell at him.

He stares back at me, looking dazed and exhausted.

As if he's about to drop.

"That creature needs locking up."

Dr. Gold appears in the stairway door. She's clearly trying to stay calm and stop herself from flying into a frenzy. She makes a move toward me, but Ria pulls us both away and holds on tight.

"You can run off and tell lies about this company, if you

must." Dr. Gold sighs, putting the facade back up. "But you'll be trying to undo hard work and a lifesaving service for people."

"What you're doing is evil," I persist, gently moving away from Ria so that I'm standing on my own two feet and facing Dr. Gold head-on. "I won't let you."

"You're no one to let me do anything," she snaps.

"You've been using me for research for the last few weeks," I fire back, and then I spin to address Adrien's father.

"Did you know what she was doing to me?" I demand of him. Staring him right in his face. "Mr. Hawkins? Did you know why she was studying me?"

His eyes dart to Ria, who stands tall and strong behind me. And his face crumples in shame.

"How could you do that to me?" I breathe, my chest tight and my voice shaking. "How could you do it to Adrien? To people like us? What made you think you could?"

"Will you stop being so melodramatic?" groans Dr. Gold, glowering at me with a thunderous expression. "No one wants to hurt you. You're not being targeted."

"You just don't think I should be who I am?"

"I don't know if you realize that people like you aren't always bundles of joy. Maybe parents want to visit their children and see their potential. Maybe children want to visit their parents and go without the heartache. I want to fix everyone! I want to make an army of perfect, well-behaved digital versions of people. Without the boring virtues or the constant need to ask why. Because wouldn't life be easier? If people who always ask questions and get in the way . . . couldn't?"

"That isn't your place," Ria says coolly.

"Oh, spare me any lectures from a stupid, spoiled rich girl," Dr. Gold retorts, smirking. "Spare me that. If I want advice on which eye cream to buy, I'll ask you, Ria."

"How are you doing it?" Ria asks, her tone cool and indifferent. She is refusing to rise to the insults.

Dr. Gold smirks. "A nice digital lobotomy."

I think of my Gram and feel sick. She was made fully like me. She just hadn't been "fixed" yet. That's why she was so scared. So desperate to warn me.

She knew something terrible was coming. Knew before I did.

I turn back to Magnus. "Wasn't I a good friend to Adrien, Mr. Hawkins? Wasn't he wonderful? Wasn't everything happier?"

Silence hangs in the air for a moment before Magnus whispers, "Yes."

I feel a tear slip free and fall to the marble floor. "Then why do this to us?"

"Why are we talking to a child?" snaps Dr. Gold, addressing Mr. Hawkins while gesturing at me. "Why? She's nothing, she doesn't matter. So what if she tells a few people what we're doing? Nobody will care."

"People will care," I say steadily. Staring her down. "People aren't like you."

"No, Cora," she laughs, rolling her eyes. "People aren't like you, remember? You don't know about people."

I ignore the jibe and keep going. "You think other people are like you, but they're not. They'll see what you're doing. And they'll say it's wrong. Most people are good."

She laughs again and it echoes harshly in the large cave of a lobby. "Most people are stupid. And money talks, Cora. I'll let you in on that, money talks an awful lot. If people want me to leave their relative unchanged, that's their prerogative, but others will want a better product. And they'll pay for it too. I know lots of people who will want the secret to building the perfect Gram. Oh, they'll pay. Investors don't care about ethics, sweetheart."

"The investors don't know."

We all look to the new voice in the room and I break into a smile as Gregor appears, emerging from the Peace Garden. He stares down Dr. Gold and, for the first time ever, he really looks like our mum.

"Your investors don't know about your creepy little erasure project. If they did, it would be terrible PR."

Dr. Gold's expression is unreadable for a moment.

Her eyes flit back to Magnus.

"It wasn't meant to be like this," Magnus says brokenly. Looking around at all of us. "I never thought . . . I just wanted to not feel . . ."

"Mr. Hawkins, there was never a thing wrong with Adrien," I say, with all the compassion I have left in me. "There just wasn't. And even if there were, it's not our job to fix each other. His brain was perfect. What Gold is trying to do, it's not right. She's not turning something bad into something good. It's not like patching up a wound or wearing glasses. He never needed improving."

Magnus stares at the carpet. "If he had been concentrating, if he had been capable of focusing, he wouldn't have been hit by that car. He would be awake right now."

Seeing him close to the edge makes me want to cry. I take a step toward him, trying to draw him back into our light. "Mr. Hawkins, those men that hit Adrien. They made the choice to get behind the wheel of that car and drive like that. They made the choice to gamble with other people's lives. I saw them. Before they even hit him. Then they took off and left him. They're the ones made wrong, not him."

His knees give and he sinks to the floor. Gregor and Ria go to him and Dr. Gold lets out a noise of derision.

"This is all so tedious," she mutters. "And it doesn't matter. This is my company. My vision. I don't need any of you, and none of you have any business stopping me."

"Who am I?"

All five of us start and turn. Sitting behind her desk, staring at Dr. Gold with an open expression of horror, is Noma. The Gram. She must have heard every word and my heart cracks and breaks a little for her.

She looks exactly how I feel.

"What"—she speaks with a quiver in her voice—"am I?"

Dr. Gold stalks forward a few steps, meeting the Gram's eyes with an intensity that I know I will never achieve. "You are nothing."

Ria gasps and Gregor swears. He darts toward the desk, looking for wherever Noma's chip is located so that he can disconnect her. Stop her from processing the cruelty of it all.

"I am nothing," the Gram says softly. Gregor finds it at last and pulls.

"Nothing," Noma echoes as she begins to fade. "Nothing. Nothing."

"You are despicable," Gregor snarls at his boss. "You should be ashamed."

"Yeah, shame is for other people," Dr. Gold snaps back, typing something speedily on her mobile. "And I'm absolutely sick to death of you all. You can all go to hell. And, Cora? When your little vegetable friend does die . . . he'll be here ready and waiting. You're welcome."

She throws one last look at Magnus before staggering toward the front doors of Pomegranate. She grips the door as if she's about to fall down and then throws it wide open, stumbling out onto the sidewalk.

"Let her go," Ria says quietly. "It'll catch up to her, don't worry."

"We can't let her go," I tell the three of them, watching the black car speed out of Canary Wharf and into town. "She's going to sell Pomegranate live on air. You said it yourself earlier, Mr. Hawkins. Millions of people will be watching."

Ria and Gregor exchange glances and Mr. Hawkins walks slowly to the empty front desk. He stares up at the words printed on the wall.

Let Them Believe.
Leave Them as They Are.
Listen and Learn.

And I know what I have to do.

"Mr. Hawkins," I plead softly. "We have time. We can get to the studio. We can tell them everything."

"They'll never let you in the studio," Gregor says dejectedly. "You'd need a pass to get in. Yes, it's live, but they won't just let someone disrupt the broadcast."

"Dad watches the show every Thursday," I say loudly, trying to drown out their doubt. "He watches because Mum used to. They always have a politician and the guest. Then questions from the audience. I don't need to disrupt anything, I'll just ask a question."

"Well . . ." Gregor hesitates, clearly thinking through the whole scenario in his head.

Not realizing that we don't have time.

"We have to try," I say to them all. I feel Adrien standing

at my side, not saying "I told you so." Just pleased that I can finally see. "And we have to go now. Before she can fool everyone."

"I have an entry pass."

Mr. Hawkins speaks so softly that I almost miss his words. I spin to look at him. He turns to meet my gaze.

"I can get you in, Cora."

His words are like a key, unlocking the final door. "Thank you," I tell him. "Then we need to go. Now."

DEBATE HOUR

Gregor stays at Pomegranate to man the fort while Adrien's parents and I speed to the television studios south of the river. Ria drives. Fast but agile, every part of her calm and collected. Focused.

"I'll get you into the audience," Magnus says as we reach the side entrance to the building. "Keep your head down, look meek."

I roll my eyes but nod.

"She'll be in the greenroom," Ria says. "She won't spot you."

"Okay." I undo my seat belt as the car slows. "I just need to get hold of the microphone before she can tell any of her lies."

"Cora." Ria turns to look at me. "You have to let her speak first."

"What?"

We're out of the car now and walking briskly, with Mr.

Hawkins behind us, toward the crowd of people waiting to be let in.

"Let her lie to them," she says carefully, keeping her voice lowered. "Let her do her whole spiel. Then you can expose her."

"I don't get it." I stand between the two of them and can feel Adrien with me, telling me to listen.

"You should always let someone show who they really are, Cora."

I listen. I mull it over.

"Come on." Mr. Hawkins steers us to one side. "I know a quicker way in. And this pass is VIP, anyway."

"I don't need VIP treatment, I just need a seat in the crowd," I tell him.

"I know," he says gently. "Let me get you there, Cora." This is him making amends. And it's up to me whether I accept or not. I look at Ria Hawkins. She's smiling at me. It's a proud smile. One that feels like a balm after everything that's happened tonight.

"Okay. Let's go."

Ria and I are in the audience. At the end of a row, by the aisle. There are about a hundred people in total, and they all talk among themselves as the crew set up and prepare for the live broadcast to begin.

The host can be seen in the shadows of the set, getting a microphone attached. He looks casual, calm. Ready to do yet another weekly live show, like the hundreds he's done before.

People sometimes shout out and get passionate on this program, but I don't think I've ever seen anyone do what I'm about to.

"Are you nervous?"

Ria asks me the question softly. Her hand on the armrest between us, the rings on her slender fingers shining when they catch the studio lights.

"Yes," I answer bluntly. "I'm scared."

"Don't be," she says quickly, her voice quiet but intent. "I'm right here."

I grip her hand briefly.

"I'm here if things get ugly," she adds.

"Things are already ugly," I whisper. "People need to know."

"And I don't think you realize how much it will matter, coming from you," she responds, looking ahead at the stage as the final touches are put in place for the broadcast.

"No one ever listens to me," I scoff, a little worn out.

"Adrien did."

Hearing her say his name now, with what I'm about to do, I feel like crying.

"You're not just doing this for him, Cora," she says firmly. "You're doing it for yourself as well. And that's important. You're important."

I take a quick breath and feel the nerves catching up with me. "I really wish he could be here."

My voice breaks as I say it. I'm scared. I'm really scared.

"I know, sweetheart."

Suddenly, everyone starts to clap as the host takes his seat and the camera crew get into position. Lights find their settings.

Dr. Gold and another man walk onto the stage. They sit in the two empty chairs and I have to fight the urge to duck down in my seat, hoping she doesn't spot me here in the darkness.

"Welcome to *Debate Hour,* I'm Richard Parton. Joining me tonight, the minister of health, Elijah Warrington, and Dr. Sabrina Gold of the Pomegranate Institute. Welcome to them, our studio audience and our viewers at home."

We applaud. I do it absentmindedly, keeping my gaze fixed on Dr. Gold. She doesn't look a bit frazzled. She looks completely relaxed and utterly confident.

I don't understand how she can, but then again, I don't understand her.

Parton talks to the minister of health for the first few minutes, discussing health care policy. Warrington gives very scripted and slightly boring answers. So Parton moves quickly to Dr. Gold.

"Now, what exactly is it that you do, Dr. Gold?" he asks conversationally, turning all his attention to her. "You've written a few columns about the advancement of artificial intelligence, we all read your piece in the *Chronicle*."

I glance around, wondering who the "we" is that he's referring to.

"Well, my work is primarily focused on digital immortality."

"Quite an intense idea."

"Not really, Richard," Dr. Gold says warmly. "We've been talking about doing it properly for decades. People are already living beyond their deathbeds with their social media accounts and their online footprints. My work, what I do, allows them to properly document themselves in a collated system."

"The Pomegranate Institute."

"Pomegranate." Dr. Gold sighs contentedly, as if saying the name of her company anchors her. "At Pomegranate, we have the technology and resources available to let people and their families live on with AI. Digital uploads of their souls. We call them Grams. We do celebrities, too. Ever wanted to meet Marilyn Monroe, Richard?"

"Well . . ." Parton laughs reluctantly. He's charmed. "Of course. But let's talk about the first part. People have their, what did you say, their souls uploaded?"

"Souls, minds, yes. Whatever you want to call the essence of a person. We create digital copies and allow that person to live forever. We interview them extensively, study them, and then our incredible team re-creates them so that they can visit with their family after they pass."

"Does the person get to approve their finished product?"

Dr. Gold pauses and then smiles broadly. "We never have complaints."

"That's a lie."

People murmur and turn their heads and I realize that I'm standing and that I spoke the words loudly and sharply. A camera swings to capture me and Parton looks at me with astonishment. A boom mike is hurried over to hover above my head.

And Dr. Gold and I stare at each other.

"My name is Cora Byers," I go on, tilting my chin so that the fluffy microphone can catch every word. "I'm twelve years old, nearly thirteen. My mum died a year ago. I thought Pomegranate was the greatest thing I'd ever heard of."

I take a breath and fight the urge to turn back. I stare at Gold.

"I thought she was the greatest."

I still feel Adrien beside me. The real Adrien. I can't see him, but I can feel him. Telling me to be brave.

"Dr. Gold has been interviewing me for weeks as part of her work for Pomegranate. She and another scientist, Dr. Connelly, have studied me and worn me out with their questions and their tasks. I did this willingly because they told me my participation would help Pomegranate."

The room is uncomfortably silent. I know some people are embarrassed, and many are intrigued. This show may often get rowdy or lively, but I'm well aware that what I am doing is nothing close to normal.

But I don't care. "I'm different."

I let that sink in. Someone coughs and a few people stir. The old me would have worried. Panicked about what is going through their heads. What do they think of me; how should I act to make sure everyone knows that I'm normal and good?

But now? Again, I don't care.

"Dr. Gold told me she needed my help in order to get Grams of neurodivergent people just right."

"What is going on?" someone whispers behind me to their friend, who shushes them. A couple of producers have their heads together, but everyone else is watching me with tight attention. Even Dr. Gold is frozen in her chair.

"She studied my best friend, Adrien, as well. A year ago. She made a Gram of him."

I pause. I know what I'm about to do. I know it will change everything. The camera is fixed on me and I know that there are millions of people on the other end of it, watching live on television and later on the internet. I have to be careful.

I feel like I'm walking on a great frozen lake. I take a step and feel the ice crack and crackle beneath my foot. On the other side, I can see Adrien. Standing strong in support.

And behind me, I can feel all other kids like us. All different, all individuals. But all people that Dr. Gold thinks less of. People she thinks she needs to perfect.

I have to make sure this lake is safe for those other kids. I have to.

As I take another step, the ice hisses and cracks again. I could go plummeting into the freezing-cold water at any moment. I might not be able to haul myself up or break free from the depths.

But at least then they would know it isn't safe.

I have to do this. I can't allow her to bewitch people into letting kids like me and Adrien be altered.

"She made him wrong. She took out the parts of him that made him great. She changed him. And she is planning to do the same to everyone who doesn't fit her idea of normal."

There is murmuring in the crowd.

"Cora." Dr. Gold speaks slowly, her mouth smiling but her eyes fierce. "We've talked about this. You're mixed up. You've got it all wrong."

"No," I say calmly. "I haven't."

I look around at all the faces of the adults in the audience. Their eyes dart between Dr. Gold and me, but a few look steadily at me with a strange sort of appreciation. Not everyone, but a few. And I can tell that they are listening.

"My friend Adrien is asleep," I say, and it stings. I feel tears prickle. "He feels gone. They don't think he's coming back. But Dr. Gold knew I wasn't ready to let go. She said she would let me visit with the Gram that she made of him, if I let her study me for her department. She took advantage of everything I was feeling, and she will do the same to everyone else. Pomegranate will target people who are grieving and give them a false promise."

"Young lady, these are some grave allegations," Parton suddenly butts in, eyeing his producers as he does.

"They are," I acknowledge. "What Pomegranate plans to do is unethical. And I think people have the right to know."

"What do you say to these comments, Dr. Gold?"

Dr. Gold drags her gaze from me to Parton, all charisma and warmth gone. She looks like she's just walked free of a fire.

"The child is delusional, sadly," she eventually manages to state.

"So you deny all that?" Parton pushes, glancing fleetingly at me. "I must say, this is a first. We're used to opinionated audience members on this show, but never one quite this young."

A small pulse of amusement beats in the room, but it dies quickly.

"Of course I deny all that," Dr. Gold says swiftly. "She's completely misunderstood what we do. At Pomegranate, people will be re-created exactly as they were in life. Warts and all."

"Lies," I maintain.

"I must say, when I was first introduced to Dr. Gold and the Pomegranate Institute," Warrington, the politician, says, joining the argument, "none of this was mentioned. I think the little girl is mistaken; we were briefed on the AI program and were assured that no alterations or interferences would occur."

Dr. Gold nods heartily but I can see that she is a little rattled by his intervention. He has just told everyone watching that she pitched Pomegranate as an inclusive and ethical operation.

"What if I have proof?" I call out boldly.

The ice beneath me cracks further, but I'm ready to swim. I'm ready to fight.

"Proof?" Dr. Gold scoffs, but her voice breaks as she does.

For the first time, a little ripple of doubt passes over her face.

"I'm not doing anything wrong," she states, but it doesn't sound quite as confident. "I'm like a plastic surgeon, I'm correcting the undesirable parts of people."

"No," I say firmly, not allowing her to manipulate the room anymore. Not allowing her to lie about what is really going on. "People choose to get surgery. It's their personal choice. What you're doing is the equivalent of tricking people and forcing them into getting parts of them deleted because you happen to think that they are less than.

Well, that's your opinion, Dr. Gold. It isn't fact. If I had money and power and decided I wanted to get rid of people I didn't like, that wouldn't make me superior or better. It would just make me a monster."

There are a few whispers and gasps around the room as we glare at each other, the two men onstage looking utterly perplexed and unsure of what to do.

"I have every right to be here. As me. Exactly as I am," I say, full of defiance and confidence that I never imagined I could have. Full of the courage and the right to stand squarely against her. "I might be different from you, I might be different from every person in this room, but you have no more of a right to exist than I do. You don't get to pick and choose which bits of me are fine. All of me is fine."

Dense, incredulous silence.

"Cora." She looks at me and, for the first time tonight, the old Dr. Gold reappears.

The one that isn't real.

"Cora. Be honest. If someone came along and said they could take your disability away . . . You would, wouldn't you?"

I smile at her. And reach into my pocket. The same pocket I reached into earlier tonight.

And I show her my recorder.

All the color pours out of her face, like water running speedily down a drain. As she realizes that every word we have exchanged this evening, prior to coming here, is recorded on the device.

"You did say I would make a great reporter one day," I tell her.

I present the device to the camera and show the whole room. I hold it high, like a beacon.

"Everything I have said tonight is proven on this recording," I declare.

People are talking now, loudly. One producer runs out of the studio, presumably to get someone more important.

Ria squeezes my hand in encouragement, so I keep going.

"Do you know who the Turing Test is named after, Dr. Gold?"

Recognition sparks in her eyes, as well as a little fear. "Alan Turing."

"Yes. Did you know he was like me?"

She gives nothing away, her face empty. But I don't mind.

"They beat him down. Wore him down. For being different. But you know what? I will always exist, Dr. Gold. Long after I'm gone. You can't erase people like me. You can't touch what we are. For too long, people like you have tried to work out how to erase some of the best minds to have existed on this planet. Because you're scared. You can't control them."

I remember every word Adrien said that night of the dance. I feel the indignation he showed then. Now in my own veins, pulsing through me and moving me onward. He was right. I am dangerous. But for all the best reasons.

"A scientist at Pomegranate once asked if I knew what love was. At the time, I was so insulted by the question, I didn't know what to say. But now I do. Love is accepting and celebrating something or someone for every natural fiber of them. The parts that they can't change . . . those are the parts that need loving the most."

A memory of Adrien and me dancing in the middle of the school hall, completely uncaring of the judgment and bemusement being projected at us, flashes in my mind. When neither one of us bothered with other people's opinions. I think that was the happiest I've ever been.

I look out at them all, eyes wet and hands trembling. Then I look to Dr. Gold. Everyone in the room can hear me, but I speak only to her.

"I love my brain. I love being me. I know who I am, Dr. Gold. It took my whole life to get here. And that's none of your business."

More murmurings and a producer quickly whispering something in Parton's ear, off camera. I continue to hold up the recording device, gripping it with relief and triumphant pride.

"Recordings aren't admissible," Gold breathes, her

eyes locked onto my recorder. As if she's thinking of snatching it. Regretting ever giving it to me. "That's entrapment. They're not admissible in court."

"No, they're not," Ria chimes in, stepping up next to me and wrapping one arm around my shoulders. "But they're very illuminating if leaked online. Or published in a newspaper. And this stupid, spoiled rich girl has stupid, spoiled parents. One is a member of Parliament and the other is a newspaper editor."

Dr. Gold looks as if she might collapse. She stares at me in betrayal. Meanwhile, Warrington's face comes alive in recognition. "Ria Hawkins!"

He makes a twisted, strangled noise as he starts to put the whole picture together. Dr. Gold glances from him to Adrien's mother in confusion, clearly wondering how a woman she respects so little could cause such a reaction in a cabinet minister.

"Oh, you thought my husband was the one with all the influence?" Ria asks sweetly. "No, dear."

"And you didn't give your employees much privacy at Pomegranate, according to my brother," I add. "What with the cameras in every single room. So that's more evidence and plenty of witnesses."

She looks at us, her frantic eyes never knowing which one of us to settle on.

"Don't worry, Dr. Gold," I say calmly. "I'm used to being underestimated. And hey, if I've misread the situation . . . I'm sure someone out of the many people who are about to learn your secrets will let me know."

"You . . . ," she murmurs, staring at me, searching for a word that never comes.

I stare right back, completely defiant. "Me."

"I would like to make it clear," the politician says into his lapel, where his microphone is fixed, "that I never thought the Pomegranate Institute was a good idea, and I told the prime minister as much."

Dr. Gold's lip curls into a snarl. "You serpent."

Warrington leans away from her, eyes downcast and brow a little sweaty, but he doesn't retract his words. She throws one cursory glance at me before fixing a bright smile on her face and addressing the audience. Both the people in the room and the invisible faces on the other end of the camera.

"I believe in Pomegranate," she says maternally. "I built this company so I could allow people to live forever. Allow their families to see them again. I gave this sad little girl the opportunity to do both of those things. I made a Gram of Adrien Hawkins. Before his tragic, untimely accident. And I allowed her to meet him all over again."

"You took away everything that made him great," I bite out, taking a step toward her and casting my voice out like a life belt. "Don't stand there and pretend you're making people as they are."

"No, I'm making them better!" she yells. "I'm providing

a service. Get the true potential of a person without their defects."

"Defects?"

A woman in the front row speaks. Parton opens his mouth as if he's about to try to wrangle the room back into his control. But his exhale tells us all that he knows this isn't possible.

The cameras turn to the woman and I notice as the lights focus on her that she's a wheelchair user.

"Sheyda." She identifies herself into the boom microphone that is rushed to hover over her. "I'm a teacher. What do you actually mean by defects?" she asks calmly. "Because you're not being clear."

"Well." Dr. Gold looks Sheyda up and down and beams, giving what I'm sure she considers to be a sympathetic smile. "My technology could allow you to live forever with complete use of your legs. It would cure you."

I feel Ria's arm tighten around me.

"How dare you?" Sheyda says quietly, and people murmur. "It's not for you or anyone to say what my defects are."

I nod, relief pulsing through me.

"My daughter has ADHD," a man at the back shouts down to the stage. "You going to mess with her brain as well? You'll have to go through her mother and me first!"

"Look . . ." Dr. Gold's voice quivers slightly as she takes in the room. She and I both realize at the same time that I'm not alone. Many people in this audience are angry. Some outraged. And plenty more will be curious to hear every word that I've recorded on the device she once gave me.

She didn't count on there being people like Adrien and me in the audience.

People never do. I'm not alone.

"I'll give people the choice," she says, her tone making it sound like a compromise. A wheedling bargain, rather than a statement. "Okay? I'll give people the option of whether they want to correct themselves or not."

The room continues to get rowdy as people object. She's lost control. As the voices grow louder, she looks back to me.

"I gave you your friend back," she snaps, glaring at me. "And this is how you thank me?"

"You didn't give me anything back," I say, causing the crowd to quiet a little. "You didn't even give me a ghost. Or a shadow. You merely broke my heart all over again and gave me a false promise."

"You changed my son."

We all stare at Ria Hawkins, who looks taller and more impressive than I've ever seen a person look.

"You took something precious and wiped out the shine. And you did it without asking him."

Dr. Gold regards Ria Hawkins coolly and then rolls her eyes.

"The only thing you understand is money," I say.

"That's all. And you were so excited to charge broken, grieving people huge amounts of money for a lie. And I feel sorry for you. But I'm not going to let you hurt people who are mourning. And I'll never stand by and let you 'correct' people like me. I'm just fine as I am."

"You wouldn't want to be cured?"

Mr. Parton asks the question, gazing up at me with curiosity and polite skepticism.

"I'm not ill, Mr. Parton," I say calmly. "I don't need a cure. There are lots of things that need curing in the world right now. I'm not one of them."

The room settles into quiet and I feel everything at once. Not just the heavy, sweaty lights and the soupy studio air. I feel the mixed emotions of everyone in the room. Some undoubtedly taken in by Dr. Gold's talent for appearing so reasonable. Her ability to hide horrible intentions and ideals behind polite smiles and level-headed words.

I feel Adrien, the real Adrien, with me. Reminding me that I'm doing the right thing.

"Not everyone will feel like me," I tell the room. And everyone watching at home. "Some people might want to change who they are. But that's a choice for them to make. Not their families. Not people like her. Not even you, Minister."

The minister of health looks up, startled and twitchy.

"I don't like my eczema," I add. "I'd probably choose

to get rid of that, if I had the option. My dad would give up his arthritis. My mum . . . she fell ill. She would have given anything to cure what she had. But I'm not unwell. I don't have an illness. I would never give up being autistic. It's woven into me. It touches every thought. It's not a disease or something that needs a cure. And . . ." I suddenly think of Mum and me, and how quiet the car ride was after I was diagnosed. We never did speak easily when we were together.

But after I was given the words to explain why I felt different from other people, she just said, "Well. That's that, then. You're just you."

And somehow, it was never a problem.

Mum and Adrien aren't here. No Gram, no matter how true to life, will change that. I see that now.

But I'm here. I'm still here. And I can't keep them alive with false memories. The imperfect parts are some of my favorite parts.

Mum's death wasn't a lesson for me to learn. Adrien's accident is not a rite of passage. They aren't hurdles to jump over. They shouldn't become chains that weigh me down, even if that's what they feel like for a little while.

They're only gone if I never speak of them ever again. If I never think of them fondly. Never laugh at memories of Adrien chasing his dog and trying to make him wear human shoes.

I won't feel this way forever. And I will never be the only person to feel this. Every person I pass in the street, every friend I will make in the future. They will all know. Now or someday.

And we can talk about it. Together.

"And I'm still learning how to be in this world," I add, feeling Adrien's faraway pinkie linked with my own. "And I really wish my best friend were here with me. And I wish my family were whole. But as much as that, I wish people would realize that they don't get to decide who is worth keeping as they are and who needs correcting. Maybe if people like me were actually allowed to speak for ourselves, you would know not to mess with us. Well. Dr. Gold told me tonight that people wouldn't stop her from making money with Pomegranate. She told me people weren't like me, that they wouldn't agree with me. That they all think like her."

I fix my former mentor with my sternest look. I've done it. I explained myself. The words came out, exactly as I needed them to. I'm being heard.

"I really hope you all prove her wrong," I say to the rapt audience.

Dr. Gold's face twists in fury and then the whole room descends into pandemonium. A producer is trying to lure me onto the stage, a body mike ready, and the audience is starting to fire questions and comments at the panel. But I've got something more important to do. I promise the audience I will release all recordings to the press and meet with government ministers at a later date. I've done what I came here to do, I've reached the other side of the lake.

And now I have someone I need to say goodbye to.

THE WAITING ROOM, AGAIN

Ria, Gregor and I stand before the Waiting Room with the blue door.

"I can't go in," whispers Adrien's mother. "But when it's done. When it's over, bring his chip out to me."

"I'll bring the chip out now," Gregor says gently. "He'll last on the drive until Cora has said goodbye. And then, after the chip is destroyed, he'll be gone for good. Are you sure you want to do this?"

I look to her. It's her decision.

"I'm sure," she says serenely. "I am."

"All right then," says Gregor. "I'll wake him up and bring the chip out. You'll have time, Cora."

I nod. Gregor slips in and Ria walks down the corridor, taking a moment to herself. I focus on breathing. When Gregor reappears, he's carrying the chip.

"You have time. Go on in," he says kindly, pulling me into a quick hug.

I hold on until he lets go. Then I step inside.

Adrien looks up as I appear. We just stare at each other for a moment.

"Where have you come from?" he asks, tilting his head to the right as he tries to read me.

"A big old mess," I say honestly, laughing in a rocky way. "Long story."

"I've got time."

I smile wanly. "No. You don't."

I sit down across from him and wish more than ever that I could grab his hand.

"I feel . . ." He glances around the Waiting Room. "I feel like all I have is time."

I lay my hands in my lap and take a moment of stillness for the first time tonight. "I never feel like I have enough time."

"You can have some of mine."

I laugh. And laugh a bit more. "God, what a night."

"Tell me."

"Everything got a bit too grown-up for a spell."

"Nothing worse than that."

"Right?"

I chuckle. I sit back in the comfortable seat, knowing it's the last time I ever will.

"Talk to me about something?" I ask.

"What do you want to hear?"

"Doesn't matter." I close my eyes. "Anything."

"Well . . ." I can tell he's thinking. In whatever capacity he's been given. "It gets lonely here sometimes."

"Lonely?"

"Yeah. But then I remember that you'll come and visit."

"Adrien"—I sit up and open my eyes—"I don't want you to be lonely anymore."

He meets my gaze, and for a moment, I fall under the spell again. Believing it's real, feeling the fireflies of happiness inside that soar freely when you're with your best friend.

"What is this place?" he asks faintly.

"It's . . ." I pause. I would be lying if I said I hadn't thought about telling Adrien's Gram everything. About telling him the truth of his existence. Or lack thereof. But now that I'm in front of him again, feeling the vulnerability, I know it's not the right thing to do. I don't want that for him.

"You're in a waiting room," I whisper. "You're just waiting to go in."

"Oh." He settles ever so slightly. "Okay."

"I'll tell you about my best friend," I say warmly. "If you like."

"Sure."

"Well, he had ADHD. And it made him brilliant. Really bright and brilliant. And he loved flying, used to take flying lessons so that he could be a pilot when he grew up. He loved all sorts of food, even the spiciest kinds that make my mouth catch fire."

He laughs.

"And he had a dog. Who was always trying to keep him out of trouble."

"I have a dog," he says eagerly. "But . . . I don't know where he's gone."

"It's okay," I say quickly. "It's all okay."

"What else?"

"He actually had quite a good singing voice," I say, giggling. "He would roll the windows of the car down and hang out the side like a dog and sing so the whole of London could hear. Opera, sometimes. And it made me almost pee with laughter."

He snorts, a hauntingly familiar sound.

"And he was an amazing dancer. Silly, but amazing. He gate-crashed my school dance because he knew I'd be anxious and left out. He got the whole room stomping around in a massive conga line."

His face is wide and warm as he watches me tell my stories. I drink it in.

"I'm autistic," I say, proud and unapologetic. "And sometimes, I'd get overstimulated or a bit grumpy. And he wouldn't badger me or blame me. He would just link his pinkie with mine and say nothing at all. And it always made everything better."

He looks down at his hands and I wonder if he knows. That they're just code. He holds out his pinkie and, after a small hesitation, I hold out mine.

They link but I don't feel a thing. Not physically, at least.

"What happened?" he asks.

I stare at my best friend. His exact image. Every inch, every pore exactly as I remember. The voice so similar, it's like talking to a specter.

"He's in a coma," I tell him. "He was hit by a car. They don't think he'll wake up."

He stares at me and I stare back, my smile tired and my eyes wet.

"I'm really sorry."

The real Adrien wouldn't have said sorry, he'd have sworn and said it was all horrible, but it's somehow okay.

"I miss him all the time," I go on, feeling every emotion of the evening flood through me and sink into my bones. I'm exhausted. "There's no other way to say it. But I need to stop thinking that he's still here. He isn't. Not really."

Because trying to move on from Adrien sometimes feels like striking a match, watching it burn down and then frantically searching for another to light. Eventually the box will be empty, and I will be left in the darkness.

I need to be in the light again.

"I bet he misses you too."

I glance up at him, surprised. He's looking at me with an almost knowing expression. One that scares me.

I lean forward a little and make sure not to look at the clock on the wall. Or even the mirror.

I think about all the things people like to say when someone passes away. That they're not in pain anymore. That they're in a better place.

But I don't know a better place than this. Alive. Here.

I know that sadness was blurring my vision when it came to the Grams. Grief is like rain. When you're standing in the street, drenched and freezing cold, it's hard to remember what it's like to feel warm and dry. It's hard to imagine feeling warm and dry ever again.

But some people are umbrellas. And they keep away the worst of the storm.

I fall into the illusion one last time. "What do you think heaven is like?"

He ponders my question. "I'm not sure."

"Do you think it's really lovely or is it like this?" I ask. "Like a waiting room?"

"It's not like this," he says confidently. "You get to look back down whenever you want, but never enough to make you sad. All your favorite foods are there and they're all good for you. Your favorite music plays but you never get bored."

I smile. Whenever Adrien found a new song he liked, he would put it on repeat and listen to it one hundred times in a row. Until it was embedded in him.

"Do you think we change?" I press gently. "When we arrive?"

"What do you mean?"

"I mean, do you think we become perfect? Do you think we have to be perfect to get in?"

He grins and déjà vu rushes through me like a river of memories.

"No way. Definitely not. We're the same as we were. The same as we are."

I smile through tears. "That's what I think too."

"We don't have to see the people who bothered us down here," he goes on, taken with the subject. "They're in a different area. No drama, we're with the people who love us. And everyone has time for everyone."

"Yes."

"And people can work doing what they love. Or not."

"Is it like a little village?"

"No," he says softly. "More like a party. You can mingle and talk to the people you want, but you can also go and be by yourself. Or go and sit with a friend in the garden."

I make a small sound and look down quickly, hoping he doesn't see.

"That does sound good. A garden does sound like heaven."

He smiles encouragingly at me. "Your best friend would be there. Waiting."

"Would he?"

"Yeah." He looks down at his pinkie once more. "I promise."

And then his pinkie starts to disappear. Begins to fade.

"Adrien," I say quickly.

"Yes, Cora?"

We look at each other and I let everything I cannot say show on my face.

"Everything is going to be okay, Adrien."

He nods. "I'm going somewhere new, aren't I?"

My jaw trembles hard, harder when I try to stop it. "Yes."

"Okay." He looks at his hands as they start to vanish into the air. "Hey, Cora?"

"Yes?"

He looks into my eyes and all the code vanishes and I'm looking at my best friend. My best friend in the whole world.

"Take care of my mum, please."

"I will." I sniff violently and laugh at myself. "I will, Adrien. She loves you so much, we all love you so much."

He beams at me. This strange but wonderful ghost.

This manufactured echo of my dearest friend.

"Hey, Cora. I always did like that name. Don't worry about me," he says brightly, smiling like he always did when he was about to start a new adventure. "I'm going over the clouds."

I let out a surprised sputter of laughter and nod passionately. "Yes, you are, Adrien. You are."

His eyes lock on mine as the last of him starts to disappear. "Goodbye, Cora."

"Goodbye, Adrien."

And as suddenly as he came into my life, in a garden when I was angry and lonely and scared . . . he leaves. And I feel strong. And capable. And myself.

Even if the pain of losing him forever hurts more than anything I've ever known.

I feel it all. I'm not numb, I feel everything. And I put it aside to say thank you to an empty room.

Because now he's free.

MOVE ON

Everything got better.

Gregor carefully broke Adrien's chip into two halves, on Ria's request, and we each took one half. I wear mine on the end of a necklace and keep it against my heart. We also found the book with all the other chips. I destroyed mine with a hammer. It was very cathartic.

Then we called the family members of every other chip. Told them the truth. Asked them if they wanted the chips destroyed.

They all said yes.

Adrien's grandmother ran a deep exposé in her paper on Pomegranate. Mr. Hawkins spoke to the paper about his involvement and his regret about the project. It was raised in Parliament. The whole world watched and people all over the globe were astonished and horrified. A movement grew. One that said no to digital eugenics.

All kinds of disabled people and their families protested

peacefully in the streets. While a part of me had always felt alone, always felt afraid that I really was getting it all wrong like Dr. Gold tried to have me believe, seeing them put everything into perspective. It became about choice. Our choice over how we define ourselves, and our choice to stand out in a world that had tried to make us disappear.

I wasn't alone. I had never been alone.

Many female scientists came out to denounce Dr. Gold. Some had stories of unethical things she had done as early as her first year of university. Some of them invited me to speak with them, others wrote beautiful letters that I pinned to my bedroom wall.

They were real. They were everything I had been searching for.

Now, as I stand outside the Royal Courts of Justice in London, I think of the summer that has gone by since my time at Pomegranate began.

I started a campaign to raise the voices of neurodivergent people, speaking openly about my experience at Pomegranate. And Adrien. I told the whole world about him, in all the cities he wanted to visit. I brought him with me.

"Cora?"

It's Dr. Connelly. I've just come out of the courtroom. This is the day Pomegranate will finally die, as it pleads its case to the world for one last time. Then it will be banned forever.

"Dr. Connelly," I say curtly, taking him in.

"This whole thing is so unfortunate," he babbles, looking around the throng of people in the large lobby of the old building. "I was never fully aware of what they were really doing."

I hardly believe that, but I don't attack him. I just feel sorry for him.

"It was ridiculous, really," he says, getting too close and too flustered. "Ridiculous. I didn't know what I was doing."

"Don't worry, Dr. Connelly," I say, smiling. "You're not a ridiculous person. You're just a person . . . with ridiculousness."

He stares for a moment and then seems to turn a little purple. I turn away, ready to see if Dad and Gregor are nearby and ready to head home. I've done my part, I've given my account. I feel better for it.

I glance over at a crowd of journalists, all pointing their microphones toward a woman with vibrant red hair and bold lipstick. I feel a little star-struck. Since starting my campaign against Pomegranate, I've come to realize there are so many more people like me out there than I knew.

Clara Linell, an autistic lawyer, is fielding questions.

"You were the first autistic attorney to come out against Pomegranate," one reporter says loudly.

"The first openly autistic attorney," corrects Clara, a little irritably. "We have been among you all for hundreds of years, don't forget. But yes, I'm proud to stand against that vile operation and I look forward to today's proceedings. I don't believe we shall have to hear from them ever again, after this. Gold is an opportunist. They come along every now and then and try to stretch decency and ethics until they break. So thank God for Cora Byers."

She suddenly catches sight of me and her slightly bored expression breaks into a broad smile. I find myself returning it.

"That girl," Clara says, pointing a polished finger at me, "has more courage in her little neurodivergent finger than anyone in that courtroom. She's saved us all from a hideous possibility. Done the work you lot should have been doing."

I can feel color creeping up my neck.

"Cora, what would you say to other autistic children right now?" one journalist shouts over the others. I swallow, nervous. Even after all the interviews, the speeches and the articles, I still sometimes worry about the power of what I do or do not say.

"I would tell them . . . however you feel about who you are is okay. It's not for other people to decide your worth or how much space you take up. It's not for them to dictate who this world is for. It's for all of us."

"What would you say to parents who do want to change their children?" another asks.

I spot Magnus Hawkins and his lawyer, over by the entrance to the courtroom. They're speaking hurriedly until Magnus digs in his pocket to answer his mobile.

"I would say, it's not your place. Sorry. It's not your body, it's not your mind. Children are not extensions of their parents; they are their own people."

I watch Magnus suddenly grab at the wall he is standing next to, trying to steady himself. I wonder what news he's just been told.

"I like who I am," I say, keeping my eyes on him. "I like what I am. It's perfectly okay if other people like me don't feel the same. But we get the final say. Nobody else."

"What would you say to the Pomegranate Institute?"

I've been asked this question so many times. But it's just the same as it was in that television studio.

"Are they monsters?" prompts one journalist, clearly digging for a headline.

I pause. Dad always says I never have to answer any of them. That I only need to speak if I want to, and if I have something to say.

And I do. I do have something to say.

"There's no such thing as monsters," I say truthfully. "We've just got to stop making monsters out of each other. Out of people who seem different. Monsters only exist if you don't ask questions. If you let your imagination make up a story that isn't true."

They all stare at me. A little stunned.

I move away from the reporters as Clara begins discussing new legislation that has been inspired by Pomegranate.

Then I spot her.

In a white pinstriped suit with dark glasses and long, glossy hair. High heels. Her roots are dark, and she looks frailer.

We watch each other from across the marble lobby. And then she makes her way over.

"You look taller."

I stare at her cautiously. "I am."

Her lip curls slightly and she looks around at the overly grand building we're in.

"Your speeches have been very impressive."

"Thank you," I tell her.

"I liked the one in Brussels. You really make me sound colorful."

"You were."

She smiles slightly. "I never should have underestimated you, Cora. You were stronger than half the people working for me. They all sang like canaries."

I stare her down. "I was strong for Adrien. Had to be."

"Yes, well."

We stand in complete stillness as the world seems to pass by around us, loud and impersonal.

"I'm strangely proud of you," she finally says. "If I'm allowed to say that. You proved everyone wrong. And I meant what I said. You really will make a good reporter. Got the whole world listening. I read about it in the paper. Just as I said I would." She smiles grimly, something fragile passing over her face for a flash of a second. "Wasn't lying about that."

I raise my chin and speak gently. "I don't ever want to see you again, Dr. Gold."

She looks at me. For a long time. And I don't try to read her expression, because it will probably be a lie.

"Well," she breathes faintly. "Goodbye, Cora."

I watch her leave for a moment and then, "Wait!"

She stops. Turns.

"Why did you call it Pomegranate?" I ask. Remembering my Gram. The words she used. "Was it because of the myth? Fruit of the dead?"

The corners of her lips twitch. "Nah. 'Apple' was taken."

That's not the truth. We both know it. I can't see her eyes behind the dark shades, but I allow her one last lie.

And she's gone. Heading into the courtroom, soon swallowed up by the chattering crowd.

I take it all in for a moment. And then cast her away.

Like a rope that's holding a boat to the shoreline.

A rope I don't need or want.

Pomegranate is shamed on the world stage. I take no joy in it, only relief. Relief that people will be spared from her designs. Her vision, as she called it.

I have three missed calls from Gregor and Dad, which means they're waiting outside in the car. I smile and make for the exit. I wave to them when I see their faces and jog down the steps.

It's been a wildly busy few weeks since *Debate Hour* aired and the story exploded. So many engagements.

We've been invited to a late lunch at Ria's house in Knightsbridge. It's just her house now that she and Mr. Hawkins are no longer together.

I'm starting school again soon and when I think of the time when I was upset about the newspaper, I have to laugh.

"Get in, trouble," Gregor says as I reach the car.

I'm about to when I hear someone yell my name from the doors to the court. I turn and shield my eyes against the midday sun.

It's Magnus Hawkins. He's waving frantically and yelling, but it's difficult to hear over the central London noise.

"Have you heard?" he bellows.

I shake my head and get into the car. I appreciate that he's trying to make amends, but I don't have to be around him to see it.

"I'm a little nervous about Ria's cooking skills," I tell Dad and Gregor as we set off for Knightsbridge.

"She's rehired Bella." Gregor turns around in his seat to tell me.

"Thank goodness," I laugh.

I nap in the car, exhausted by the day's proceedings. Dad parks and I jolt awake. Gregor is smiling at me as he opens the car door.

"Hi, gorgeous," Ria calls from the front door of her house. She looks incredible, natural color in her cheeks again. "Go and wait in the garden, we're eating there today. Want to enjoy the last of this beautiful sunshine before the leaves fall. Now, boys." She addresses my dad and brother. "Come inside and help us carry all the food out."

"Yes, ma'am," says Dad, winking at me.

"Go," Gregor says softly, tapping my cheek once with the tip of his finger. "We'll be along in a bit."

I shake my head. They're acting stranger than usual. But I slope off around the house to reach the garden. I still have my key. I never let it go.

I pause upon reaching the gate. Cerby is waiting there, ears pricked up and eyes bright.

"Hey, boy," I murmur, smiling.

As I slip my key into the lock, I take a moment to breathe.

It's been a very strange six months. Since Pomegranate came into my life. Walking a lonely path by yourself, one that no one else has ever walked before, is only scary before you begin. Once you're walking the road, you just have to make sure that you never glance back. Never let people's incredulity, their judgment, their doubt or their hate creep in.

I step into the garden.

Sometimes, you have to show people the world you want to live in. Have to show them how you want to be treated. And then other people like you will see your footsteps upon the path and know that they can walk it too.

I catch sight of something new in the garden. A vegetable plot with soil and, presumably, planted greens. I wonder if Ria has discovered a love of gardening.

I look ahead and spot a picnic blanket laid out in the middle of the grass. The sun hits it, breaking through the trees.

And then my whole world goes away.

Someone rises, shakily, from their place by the picnic blanket. They're using a crutch to steady themselves. They lean heavily upon it as they step out of the shadows and into the baking sun.

I know I'm making some kind of noise. A loud, gasping sound. I glance up at the sky, looking for the lights. The artificial projection. The trickery.

But there's no trick. Not this time.

"Cora," he says as he reaches me. Taller than me. Only

a little calmer than me. His eyes are wet, even if they're happy. "It's me."

The key falls onto the grass, my hand no longer able to grasp it. I reach a shaking hand out to touch, to feel. I close my eyes at the last minute, expecting my hands to touch air. To break the hologram.

Instead they touch skin. Warm skin with blood pumping and life pulsing like electricity itself.

I've been so careful over the last month, with my words. Prepared, cautious. Direct. I've practiced and perfected formal answers, speeches and what to say when presented with a change of course.

All that is gone now. I feel twelve years old again.

I feel young.

And my ability to say smart, grown-up things is gone. "You're my best friend." It's all I can manage, gasping for air and trying to let my lungs catch up with my heart. "You're my best friend."

His hand closes over mine, pressing it to his face. "I know."

"Where did you go? I never thought I'd see you again."

"Wherever it was, here is better."

"You were right," I say. Because it's what I've wanted to say for months. "About Pomegranate. About everything. You were right about everything."

His face morphs into a mischievous grin. "Yes! That's what I woke up from a coma to hear. I can die now."

"Don't!" I blurt out. "Don't even joke about it."

The laughter fades from his face and he looks at me seriously. "Hey, Cora."

"Hey, Adrien."

I'm hugging him. It's real. There's nothing digital about it. It's the realest thing I've felt in months.

"When did you wake up?"

"About a month ago," he answers, still hugging me.

"A month!"

"Yeah. I've been doing rehab and occupational therapy, and stuff. Grace says hello. She told me you visited."

"I did."

"Mum wanted to tell you immediately, but I was watching you on the television every day. You were amazing. Are amazing. Telling the whole world about what they were doing. I didn't want to take you away from all that, not when it's so important."

"You are more important," I bark, squeezing my eyes tight shut to stop more water.

"No, I'm not. You were out there saving the world, Cora. I didn't want you worrying about me. And every time you did me proud, I said, 'If Cora can do all that, I can get out of bed and walk today.' I came home last night."

When Ria called to invite us to lunch.

Only, now I see a basket of food and drink by the blanket. For two. She must have food for Dad and Gregor at the house. Must've planned for this reunion to be private.

"I'm so proud of you," he says, his voice cracking. "You showed all of them. You did it for all of us. You brought that place down."

"I had to."

"I know."

I finally break away from the hug and look around the garden. Calm, tranquil and peaceful. Real peace. Not manufactured. I glance back toward the gate and smile.

"Nice vegetable plot."

"I know! Mum put it in for me. It's going to help me with my rehabilitation."

"How?" I laugh.

"No idea, but the doctor suggested it. Said vegetables are a must for healthy living so I'm going to grow my own."

I move jerkily to the blanket and sit down, not trusting my legs to keep me standing. I help him lay his crutch down next to us and sit as well.

"Not sure I'm going to be much of a pilot now," he says, a little bitterly.

"Adrien Hawkins," I say sternly. "You are capable of absolutely anything. Do you hear me? You woke up from a stinkin' coma! You sussed out Pomegranate and Dr. Gold long before I did. You can do anything you set that brilliantly wired mind to and don't waste my time with anything less."

He beams at me. Laughing. I laugh too.

Grief was a strange companion these last few months.

Now, as I look up at the trees, which will soon shed their leaves until they're bare and ready to start anew, it feels like I've emerged from a strange dream.

And now I get to live my life again.

"There is, uh, one other thing you should know," he says.

I look back at him. "Yeah?"

CODA

TWO WEEKS LATER

"This is the best layout we've done."

I turn to smirk at Adrien as he says it proudly, leaning on his crutch. "Adrien, this is the only layout we've done."

"I know, but it looks great."

We're in my school lunchroom. Our school lunchroom. That was the last surprise. Adrien decided he wanted to go back to school, around the same time Ria was offered a job at a magazine. Both were delighted to be moving on. Ria pulled some strings and got Adrien a place in my grade.

Adrien likes to joke about how he planned his coma neatly during the summer holidays so that he didn't have to write the beginning-of-school essay.

He still needs the odd afternoon off for occupational therapy and medical appointments but apart from that, we're always together.

We're running our own school newspaper. In opposition to Mr. Ramsey's. We've managed to cultivate quite the team; it seems Adrien wasn't the only one impressed by my summer antics.

"Looking very good," Ms. Mabuse says, peering over our shoulders at the layout. "Don't forget to actually eat your lunch, though."

Adrien salutes her and I nod, taking a bite out of my fresh, crunchy salad. Most of it from Adrien's garden.

"We still need a name for the paper," Adrien reminds me, chewing on his lettuce.

"How about the *Cabbage*?" I tease, pointing out the green in his teeth.

"How about"—he takes a sip of water—"the *Spectrum*?"

My pen hovers over the front page. "What?"

"The *Spectrum*."

"As in—"

"As in, a broad selection of different things." He's smiling knowingly at me. "All smart. All unique. All brilliant. All worth knowing."

I smile. He smiles. I present my fist. "The *Spectrum*."

He bumps it with his. "The *Spectrum*."

I don't think about Pomegranate often anymore. I've said all I need to about it. Now I just live my life. With my best friend. We go to the movies. We play with his dog. We look up at the clouds. We go to watch his uncle Max and his airplane. Adrien flies in it now that he's well enough.

And Pomegranate is a distant memory. I choose to think of better things. Of Mum. Of Alan Turing and his incredible invention. Of Dad and Gregor. Of Ria and her new career. Of Adrien and his terrible jokes.

Adrien and I walk the lonely road together now. It's not lonely anymore.

I'm not alone.

We laugh most of the time now, I've noticed. We spend hours after school working on the paper in the garden. Next to the vegetable plot.

I love to eat what we grow there. I've had enough of bad fruit.

ACKNOWLEDGMENTS

To the readers.

To Knights Of for allowing me to do this a second time. Saved my life. Again.

To Hux, for being the first person to support Addie in public and then Cora in private.

To Layla, the bookseller who is making the next generation better.

To every single spark that turned Addie into a firework. Tamsin, Harriet, Courtney, Kirsty, Louise, Emma, Miss Cleveland, Dean, Lily, Lucas, Jax, Fabienne, Ocean, Neil. All the teachers, bloggers, booksellers, and librarians who let a Scottish, autistic girl find her voice.

To the BLM Agency and to Lauren. Port in a storm. To Gavin Hetherington, an absolute mensch.

To Scott Evans and the Primary School Book Club. What a gift.

To Sarah and Bounce, for fighting like hell when the world was aflame.

To Annabelle, for being a true ally.

To Marssaié and Kay, for making the work beautiful.

To every friend who bought and read *A Kind of Spark,* even though we were separated by oceans or years.

To the Rights team, for the best news about my old home, New York.

To Robin Stevens, Cerrie Burnell, Maz Evans, Michelle Harrison, Jennifer Bell, Lisa Thompson, Susin Nielsen, Lucy Powrie, and Jenni Spangler, for being kind to a new author who, since writing her previous acknowledgments, still has not met a single other author in person. Thank you for not making me eat on my own at lunch.

To Eishar. Thank you for everything, and for standing up for me in the comment box of a copyedit.

To my extended family, for being the best cheerleaders. To Aileen, for being the first teacher on board.

To Josh. George Bailey. You can't carry it for me, but you do carry me.

To Mum. Thank you for looking after me when I was so ill. It gave me the idea for this book.

To Dad. I do everything I can so you'll be proud. Thank you for being *Spark*'s number one fan.

ABOUT THE AUTHOR

ELLE McNICOLL is a Scottish and neurodivergent writer, happily living in London. She has worked as a bookseller, bartender, blogger, and babysitter—all while writing stories for her own amusement. After completing her master's dissertation on the lack of Own Voices representation for neurodivergent children, she grew tired of the lack of inclusivity in the industry and wrote a book herself. Her first children's novel, *A Kind of Spark,* was a Schneider Family Book Award honor book and a Carnegie Medal nominee, and received a starred review from *School Library Journal,* which called it "a must-read for students and adults alike." You can find Elle online at ellemcnicoll.com.

SPEAK. EVEN IF IT'S QUIET.

TURN THE PAGE FOR A PREVIEW OF
ELLE McNICOLL'S AWARD-WINNING DEBUT.

AVAILABLE NOW!

1

"THIS HANDWRITING IS UTTERLY DISGRACEFUL."

I hear the words, but they seem far away. As if they are being shouted through a wall. I continue to stare at the piece of paper in front of me. *I* can read it. I can make out every word, even through the blurriness of tears. I feel everyone in the classroom watching me. My best friend. Her new friend. The new girl. Some of the boys are laughing.

I just keep staring at my writing. Then, suddenly, it's gone.

Ms. Murphy has snatched it from my desk and is now ripping it up. The sound of the paper being torn is overly loud. Right in my ears. The characters in the story I was writing beg her to stop, but she doesn't. She crumples it all together and throws it toward the classroom bin. She misses. My story lies in a heap on the scratchy carpet.

"Do not *ever* write so lazily again!" she shouts.

Maybe she isn't even shouting, but it feels that way.

"Do you hear me, Adeline?" I prefer being called Addie. "Not ever. A girl your age knows better than to write like that; your handwriting is like a baby's."

I wish my sister were here. Keedie always explains the things that I cannot control or explain for myself. She makes sense of them. She understands.

"Tell me that you understand!"

Her shouts are so loud and the moments after are so quiet. I nod shakily. Even though I don't understand. I just know it's what I'm supposed to do.

She says nothing more. She moves to the front of the class and I am left alone. I can feel the new girl glancing at me, and my friend Jenna is whispering to her new friend, Emily.

We were supposed to have Mrs. Bright this year; we met her briefly before the summer holidays. She would draw a little sun with a smiling face beside her name and would hold your hand if you looked nervous. But she got sick and Ms. Murphy came to teach our class instead.

I thought this new school year would be better. That I would be better.

I take out my pocket thesaurus. It was a Christmas present from Keedie. She knows how much I love using different words, and we laughed because the word "thesaurus" sounds like a dinosaur. I read different word combinations to calm down, to process the shouting and the ripping.

I find a word that I like. "Diminished."

✦ ✦ ✦

On days like this, I spend lunchtime in the library. I feel the other children in the class still watching me as we tuck in our chairs and leave the room, the school bell screeching so loudly. Loud noises make my head spin; they feel like a drill against a sensitive nerve. I walk through the corridors, practicing my breathing and keeping my eyes straight ahead. People talk so loudly to their friends, who are right next to them. They get too close, they push and clamor, and it makes my neck hot and my heart too quick.

But when I finally get to the library it's all quiet. A good kind of quiet. There is so much space, and an open window lets in a little fresh air. There is no loud talking allowed. The books are all categorized and labeled in their proper places.

And Mr. Allison is at his desk. "Addie!"

He has curly dark hair and big glasses, and he is tall and skinny for a man. He wears old sweaters. If I were to use my thesaurus to describe Mr. Allison, I would say he is kindly.

But I like to just say that he is nice. Because he is. My brain is very visual. I see everything in specific pictures, and when people use the word "nice," I think of Mr. Allison, the librarian.

"I have just the thing for you!"

I like that he never asks boring questions. He doesn't ask how my holidays were or how my sisters are doing. He just gets straight to talking about books.

"Here we go." He walks over to one of the reading tables and puts a large hardcover book down in front of me. I feel all the horrid feelings from earlier disappear.

"Sharks!"

I flip it open immediately and stroke the first glossy page. I told Mr. Allison last year that I love sharks. That they are the most interesting thing to me, even more than the ancient Egyptians and the dinosaurs.

He remembered.

"It's a sort of encyclopedia," he tells me, as I sit down with the book. "An encyclopedia is a book that tells you a lot about one subject, or one area of study. This one is all about sharks."

I nod, somewhat dazed from excitement.

"I suspect you know everything that's in there already, though," he says, and he laughs after he says it so I know that he's joking.

"Sharks don't have bones," I tell him, caressing the photograph of what I know is a blue shark. "And they have six senses. Not five. They can sort of sense electricity in the atmosphere. The electricity of life! They can also smell blood from miles away."

Their senses are sometimes overpowering. Too loud, too strong, too much of everything.

I turn the page to a large photograph of a solitary Greenland shark, swimming alone in the ice-cold water.

"People don't understand them." I touch the shark's

fin. "They hate them, actually. A lot of people. They're afraid of them and don't understand them. So they try to hurt them."

Mr. Allison doesn't say anything for a while, as I read the first page.

"You take that home with you for as long as you like, Addie."

I look up at him. He is smiling, but his eyes don't match his mouth.

"Thank you!" I make sure to put all the glad that I am feeling into my voice so that he knows I really mean it. He moves back to his desk and I become engrossed in the book. Reading is the most calming thing after an overly loud and unkind classroom. I can take my time. There is no one rushing me or barking at me. The words all follow rules. The pictures are bright and alive. But they do not overpower me.

When I am trying to sleep at night, I like to imagine diving beneath the cold waves of the ocean and swimming with a shark. We explore abandoned shipwrecks, underwater caves, and coral reefs. All that color, but in a wide-open space. No crowds, no pushing, and no talking. I would not grab its dorsal fin. We would swim alongside one another.

And we would not have to speak a word. We could just be.